Tomorrow They Won't Dare to Murder Us

by
Joseph Andras

Translated
by Simon Leser

VERSO

London • New York

This English-language edition first published by Verso 2021
First published as *De nos frères blessés*
© Actes Sud 2016
Translation © Simon Leser 2021

1 3 5 7 9 10 8 6 4 2

Verso
UK: 6 Meard Street, London W1F 0EG
US: 20 Jay Street, Suite 1010, Brooklyn, NY 11201
versobooks.com

Verso is the imprint of New Left Books

ISBN-13: 978-1-78873-871-2
ISBN-13: 978-1-78873-872-9 (US EBK)
ISBN-13: 978-1-78873-873-6 (UK EBK)

British Library Cataloguing in Publication Data
A catalogue record for this book is available from the British Library

Library of Congress Cataloging-in-Publication Data

Names: Andras, Joseph, 1984– author. | Leser, Simon, translator.
Title: Tomorrow they won't dare to murder us / by Joseph Andras ;
    translated by Simon Leser.
Other titles: De nos frères blessés. English | Tomorrow they will not
    dare to murder us
Description: First edition paperback. | London ; New York : Verso, 2021. |
    First published as De nos frères blessés by Actes Sud, 2016. |
    Translated into English from French. | Summary: "Winner of the Prix
    Goncourt pour premier roman, this is the real-life story of Fernand
    Iveton, the only "European" executed by France during the Algerian
    War" – Provided by publisher.
Identifiers: LCCN 2020041736 (print) | LCCN 2020041737 (ebook) | ISBN
    9781788738712 (paperback) | ISBN 9781788738729 (US ebk) | ISBN
    9781788738736 (UK ebk)
    Subjects: LCSH: Iveton, Fernand, 1926–1957 – Fiction. | Algeria – Fiction. |
    GSAFD: Biographical fiction.
Classification: LCC PQ2701.N368 D413 2016 (print) | LCC PQ2701.N368
    (ebook) | DDC 843/.92 – dc23
LC record available at https://lccn.loc.gov/2020041736
LC ebook record available at https://lccn.loc.gov/2020041737

Typeset in Electra by Biblichor Ltd, Edinburgh
Printed and bound by CPI Group (UK) Ltd, Croydon CR0 4YY

Tomorrow They Won't Dare to Murder Us

A NOVEL

Joseph Andras

Not a proud and forthright rain, no. A stingy rain. Mean. Playing dirty. Fernand waits two or three meters from the paved road, under the shelter of a cedar tree. They said half past one in the afternoon. Four minutes to go. That's right, one thirty. It's unbearable, this sly rain, no guts for real drops: just a petty drip, barely enough to wet the back of your neck and get away with it. Three minutes. Fernand's eyes are focused on his watch. A car passes. Is that the one? The vehicle does not stop. Four minutes late. Nothing serious, let's hope. Another car in the distance. A blue Panhard, registered in Oran. It pulls up on the shoulder—ramshackle grille, an old model. Jacqueline has come alone. She looks around as she gets out: left, then right, then left again. Here are the papers, the information's all there, Taleb's thought of everything, don't worry. Two papers, one per bomb, with precise instructions. *Between 19:25 and 19:30. Timer, 5 minutes . . . Between 19:23 and 19:30. Timer, 7 minutes . . .* He isn't worried: here she is in front of him, nothing else matters. Fernand slips the papers into the right-hand pocket of his work overalls. The first time he saw her, at a comrade's, amid hushed conversations and soft lighting, of course he took her for an Arab, this Jacqueline. Her hair is certainly dark, very dark, she has a long arched nose and full lips, certainly, but still she's not Arab, no. Rounded lids over large, dark—if hearty in laughter—eyes, black fruits now ringed by fatigue. A beautiful woman, no question. She takes two shoeboxes out of the trunk, sizes 42 and 44, it says on the side. Two? Impossible. I only brought this bag, look, it's too small to carry more than one bomb. The foreman's been watching me, he'll notice if I return with a second bag. Yes, he really will, believe me. Fernand holds one of the boxes to his ear: makes a hell of a racket, this thing, tick-tock tick-tock tick-tock, are you sure it won't . . . ? It's the best Taleb could do, but everything will be fine, don't worry, Jacqueline answers. I understand. Get in, I'll drop you a little further down. Funny name, this place, don't you think? We've gotta talk about something, Fernand tells himself, thinking that any topic will do so long as they haven't yet . . . The Ravine of the Wild Woman, do you know the legend? she asks. Not really, I forget. It's about a woman, last century—really puts the years on us, doesn't it—a woman who lost her two children in the forest up there. It was after a meal, a picnic, little blanket on the grass, springtime . . . I'm not going to paint you a picture. The poor little mites disappeared in the ravine, they were never found and the woman lost her mind, she spent her whole life looking for them, so people called her feral, wild, and she refused to speak, only uttered little cries like a wounded animal, until one day they found her body somewhere, over there, maybe, on the very spot where you were waiting for me, who knows? Fernand smiles. Strange story, for sure.

She pulls up. Get out here, this car shouldn't be seen near the factory. Good luck. He gets out of the car and waves. Jacqueline waves back and steps on the gas. Fernand adjusts his sports bag on his shoulder. Pale green, the strap lighter in color next to the drawstring opening, borrowed from a friend who uses it when he plays basketball on Sundays. Look as natural as possible. Like nothing's going on, nothing at all. For the past few days he's been taking it to work, to get the security guards used to it. Think about something else. The wild woman from the ravine, strange story that. Mo is here, ponderous nose overhanging his mustache. Everything alright? Yeah, sure, went out a bit to stretch my legs. Work wiped me out this morning. Nah, a little rain doesn't bother me, Mo, it's nothing, just a little drizzle, gonna pass any minute now, I'm telling you . . . Mo pats him on the shoulder: nothin', nothin', is this really Frenchie talkin'? Fernand is thinking about the bomb at the bottom of the bag, the bomb and its tick-tock tick-tock. It's two o'clock, the time has come to return to the machines. I'm coming, just putting my bag down, be right there, Mo, yes, see you in a sec.

Fernand glances around the yard, keeping his head still as he does so. As natural as possible. No sudden movements. He walks slowly toward the abandoned shed he scoped out three weeks ago. The factory's gas holder was inaccessible: you'd need to get past barbed wire and security guards, posted at three different points along the way.

Worse than a city-center bank or a presidential palace (not to mention that you have to strip off all, or almost all, your clothes before they let you through). Impossible, in short. And dangerous, much too dangerous, he had said to comrade Hachelaf. No deaths, that was the main thing: no deaths. Better that little storeroom where nobody ever goes. The old worker, Matahar, his mustard-colored head the texture of crumpled paper, gave him the key without the slightest suspicion—just need to take a nap, Matahar, I'll give it back to you tomorrow, don't tell the others, promise? The old man was as good as his word, والله العظيـم, I'll never say anything to anyone, Fernand, you can sleep tight. He takes the key out of his pocket, turns it in the lock, glances behind him, no one, he enters, opens the cupboard, puts the sports bag on the middle shelf, closes the door and turns the key again. Then goes around to the factory's main entrance, greets the security guard as usual, and approaches his machine tool. It's stopped raining, did you see, Mo? He did indeed, awful weather, this, been gray and doing whatever all November.

Fernand sits at his station and puts on his gloves, worn out at the seams. A contact, whose first and last names he does not know, will be waiting for him when the factory closes at seven, that is, just before the bomb goes off. That person will take him to a hideout in the Casbah somewhere, he doesn't know where exactly, and from there he will hook up with the guerrillas . . . The next day, maybe, or in a few days—not his decision. He has to wait patiently for his turn to leave, every day, at the same time as everyone else, put down his worn-out green gloves, *every* day,

4

joke a little with his friends and see you tomorrow, that's right, g'night guys, say hello to the family for me. Don't raise any suspicions: that's what Hachelaf kept telling him. Much as he tries not to, he keeps thinking about Hélène. He's not doing anything else, in fact—his brain, that three-pound brat, has a taste for melodrama. How will she react when she finds out that her husband has left Algiers and gone underground? Does she suspect? Was it such a good idea to keep this a secret? His comrades certainly thought so. The struggle forces love to keep a low profile, ideals require sacrifices, no room for soft hearts in this fight . . . Yes, it was for the best, for the smooth running of the operation.

It is almost four o'clock when someone calls him from behind. Fernand turns around in response to the question mark punctuating his name. Cops. Damn.

Before he can even think of running they seize and immobilize him. There are four of them, maybe five—the idea of counting does not cross his mind. Oriol, the foreman, stands further back. He pretends not to notice, but still, the bastard's mouth is trying not to smile, not to reveal anything, you never know, they say communists are past masters at reprisal. Three soldiers appear, airmen first class. Called to the rescue, no doubt. The factory is sealed off, we've looked everywhere and only found one bomb so far, in a green bag inside a closet, says one of them. Beardless. A kid. An infant. Asshole under a round helmet. All three have machine guns hanging from their shoulders. Fernand says nothing. What's the point? His failure is complete and his tongue, at least, has the

5

modesty to recognize it. One of the officers goes through his pockets and finds Taleb's papers. So there's another bomb. All hands on deck inside their military heads. Where is it? they ask Fernand. There's only one, it's a mistake, you already have it. The leader gives an order, take him to the Algiers central station right away. Oriol has not moved, would be a shame to miss the show. Fernand, now handcuffed, eyes him scornfully as he passes: he was hoping for a smirk at least, a mark of avowal, but there is nothing, not even an involuntary pucker. The foreman is impassive, outwardly collected, ramrod in the boots he lets the soldiers wear on his behalf. Did he rat him out? Did he see him enter the storeroom and leave without his bag? Or is it Matahar? No, the old man wouldn't. Not just for a nap, at any rate.

The van makes its way through the city. The sky is like a wet dog, puffy with clouds. Metallic winter. We know who you are, Iveton, we've got files on you, you communist fuck, you won't be so high and mighty anymore with your little kisser, Iveton, your little Arab mustache, you'll see, we're going to make you talk at the station, you better believe it, we're talented, we are, we always get our way, and believe me we're going to do whatever the fuck we want with your piece of shit communist mouth, we could force a mute to belt out an opera. Fernand doesn't respond. His hands are cuffed behind his back. He stares at the floor; a stained, worn-out gray. Look at us when we're talking to you, Iveton, you're a big boy you know, you're going to have to take responsibility for your little hobbies, you hear, Iveton? One of the officers smacks the top of his head (not the kind of violent smack that makes a cracking sound, no, a light smack, meant to humiliate rather than to hurt). Boulevard Baudin. Its archways. They take him to the station, second floor. A square room, twelve by twelve, no windows.

The shoebox is on the kitchen table. No, it's much too dangerous, don't touch it, says Jacqueline. The timer is relentless, liable to drive a person crazy in the most literal way, tick-tock. Are you sure? asks Djilali (known to the state as Abdelkader, whereas certain militants—it can get confusing—call him Lucien). Tick-tock tick-tock tick-tock tick-tock. Quite sure, actually. Jacqueline opens one of three cabinets and takes out a metallic sugar canister. Empties it and tries to fit the bomb inside. Too small—Djilali could tell just by looking.

Where's the bomb, you son of a bitch? Fernand is blindfolded with a thick piece of torn cloth. His shirt lies on the floor, shorn of most of its buttons. One of his nostrils is bleeding. A cop punches him as hard as he can; his jaw makes a faint cracking sound. Where's the bomb?

Jacqueline has wrapped the explosive device in white paper. She peels the label off the sugar canister and sticks it delicately onto the package. This should fool them if we get checked. Djilali clenches his teeth. Tick-tock tick-tock tick-tock. She buries the package in a big shopping bag, along with a few chocolate bars and some cheap soap.

Fernand is curled up on the linoleum, the back of his head cradled in his hands. A shoe kicks his right ear. Strip him naked if he doesn't want to talk. Two officers hold him up by the arms, a third undoes his belt before pulling down his pants and navy-blue briefs. Lay him on the bench there. His hands and feet are bound. I have to hold on, he tells himself, I have to hold firm. For Hélène, for Henri, for my country, for my comrades. Fernand shivers. He is ashamed of how little control he has over his body. His own body, which could betray, abandon, sell him to the enemy. It's going to blow in two hours, that's what it says on those papers you had: so, where did you stash the bomb?

Someone knocks on the door. Pounds, even. Police! Open up! Hélène instantly guesses they've come for Fernand. If they're here, though, they probably don't have him. Has he fled? What did he do? She rushes into the bedroom, grabs the dozen sheets of paper hidden in the nightstand and tears them into little pieces. Police! Open up! Sounds like drumming now. Fernand was clear: if anything ever happens to me, get rid of all of this immediately, you understand? She runs to the toilet, throws them in and flushes. A few pieces float to the surface. She flushes again.

The bomb, motherfucker, talk! Electrodes were placed on his neck, near the sternocleidomastoid muscles. Fernand shrieks out. He does not recognize his own cries. Talk! The electric current is in his flesh, burning its way down to the dermis. We'll stop when you tell us.

8

Djilali and Jacqueline reach the square. A group of nuns are walking past an old bearded man in a turban who is now crossing the street, slowly, trembling with all his years down to his wooden cane while a younger Arab, wearing a soot-brown suit, helps him along. A cacophony of cars and trolleybuses; a driver swears and strikes his door with the flat of his hand; kids are playing ball under a palm tree; a woman in a *haik* is carrying a small child, buried in her arms. Djilali and Jacqueline may not mention it, but they take note: the streets are crawling with CRS security vehicles. The first attacks claimed by the National Liberation Front have put the city on edge recently, to say the least. People don't yet call it by its name, but it is well and truly here, the *war*, the one concealed from the public under the dull word *events*. Late September, there were explosions at the Milk Bar and La Cafétéria on rue Michelet. And then again, two days ago, at the Hussein Dey station, the Monoprix supermarket at Maison-Carrée, on a bus, on a train on the Oujda–Oran line, and at two cafés in Mascara and Bougie . . . Jean lives on rue Burdeau. Djilali whispers in Jacqueline's ear that it would be better if she went in first, alone, so he can keep a lookout behind them. She pushes the door open with her grocery bag. He looks around, nothing suspicious, no police.

Open up! Hélène musses her hair and unmakes the bed. She opens the bedroom window and, pretending to yawn, apologizes to the officers down on the street, she was sleeping, she only just heard them, I'm sorry. Three Traction Avant police cars are parked in front of their house. Disdain in shining metal. There are a dozen men.

What do you want? she asks. Can't you see? We have orders to search the premises, open up immediately! I'm all alone here, I don't have to open anything, I don't know you, besides, how do I know you're the police? Hélène reckons that if something's happened to Fernand she's better off playing for time, to keep them here as long as possible. One of the officers, clearly irritated, raises his voice and orders her to open the door, otherwise they'll smash it in. What do you want? My husband? He's at the factory, go look for him there. Hélène does not budge from the window. We'll smash the door down!

Why are you covering for the fellaghas, what are they to you? Cut that shit, Iveton, come on! The electrodes are now on his testicles. A police officer, sitting on a stool, activates the generator. Fernand, still blindfolded, screams again. I have to hold, hold on. Not say anything, not let go. At least give the comrades time to hide when they realize what's happened, if they don't already know, but how could they (and what time is it anyway?), if they don't already know I've been arrested. Yes, what time could it possibly be? Why did you betray your people, Iveton?

Jean bends over the bomb. The room is dark, the lighting inadequate. Jacqueline sits on the room's only chair while Djilali returns from the kitchen with two glasses of water. Tick-tock tick-tock tick-tock. You know how to disarm it? Jean indicates his hesitation with a grimace. He's done it before, yes, but on a different model. This time he's not sure he knows the mechanism. He assesses the wires which connect the device to the timer, a Jaz brand alarm clock. Jacqueline's name is on the bomb, written in white: Taleb's homage to a militant, a sister in battle, who's been risking her life for Algeria despite being neither Muslim nor Arab—Jacqueline is Jewish. If you're not sure, don't touch anything, we don't want it to blow up in our faces. Jean offers to get rid of it far away, outside the city, somewhere deserted where it won't hurt anyone. Why not the Terrin Coalworks? suggests Djilali. Yes, that could work, it's safe over there.

We're going to shove it up your ass if you don't talk, did you hear, are you listening? Fernand would have never believed that this was it, torture, the infamous *question*. The question which requires only one answer, the same, always the same: hand over your brothers. That it could be so excruciating. No, not the right word. Our alphabet is too decorous. Horror can't but give up before its twenty-six little characters. He feels the barrel of a handgun against his stomach. Pistol or revolver? It pokes in half an inch or so beside the navel. I'm going to blow a hole in there if you don't talk. Do you understand, or do I have to say it in Arabic?

Jean has urged Jacqueline and Djilali to go back home. It's more sensible, best not be in the same place for too long. Night dilutes the city in soot, in coal; under a sated sun, the muezzin calls the faithful to prayer, اشـهد ان لا الـه الا الله; on rue de Compiègne, Jean lights a cigarette and drives straight ahead, arriving at the Chasseriau ramp, where boys are sitting on donkeys, laughing and laughing, Chasseriau . . . who was he, again? اشـهد ان محمد رسول الله, Jean glimpses a police station on his right, a CRS police van parked not too far away. Empty. After all, why not? The bomb is ready,

11

set to go off at 7:30, all he needs to do is . . . He brakes abruptly, picks up the package under his seat and gets out. Behind him, cars are honking. He runs over to the van, crazy idea really, lowers the back door handle, it's open, drivers are shouting behind him, he gets in, slides the package under one of the benches and quickly returns to his car.

Hélène has finally consented to let them in, not doubting that they might indeed "smash the door in." She rubs her eyes again and explains that she was asleep. They search every room in the house—bathroom included—and inspect every drawer, open every wardrobe, pull out the bedlinen, leave clothes strewn on the floor, return nothing to its proper place. One fat officer, more zealous than the rest, meticulously checks the food containers. Hélène, annoyed, points out that he should be more careful and respectful of others' property; the fat officer does not look up, he keeps at it, nose deep in rice and rye flour. One of his colleagues entreats him to listen to Madame Iveton and conduct the search with more restraint. A letter, guys, look, I found something! A cop proudly displays mail from Hélène's father, written in Polish. Both of them are originally Polish, in fact, and this is family correspondence, nothing more: Joseph asking after his little Ksiazek, as she was known before she came to France. And to think the police take these sentences for a coded message; Hélène smiles to herself.

Fernand's body is almost entirely burned. Every part of it, every bit, every inch of white flesh has been electrocuted. He is made to lie on a bench, still naked, head hanging backwards over nothing. One of the police officers puts a wet blanket over his body, while two others tie him securely to the bench. Your second bomb's going to blow in an hour. If you don't talk before that we're going to do you right here—you'll never see anyone again, you hear, Iveton? Fernand can finally have a look around the room: they just took his blindfold off. He has trouble opening his eyes. The pain is too sharp. His heart twitches, needles, barbs; he spasms again. Colleagues of ours are at your place right now, haven't you heard? With your little Hélène, and from what they just said over the phone she's quite a looker, your wife . . . you wouldn't want her to get hurt, would you? So you're going to tell us where the bomb is, okay? An officer puts a piece of cloth over his face and the water starts to pour. The rag sticks, he can no longer breathe, he swallows water as best as he can to try to get some air but it's no good he's suffocating his stomach swells and water flows flows flows.

Seven o'clock in the evening. The unknown contact, Yahia, the one Fernand was supposed to meet after work, is waiting by the factory. He has borrowed a car for the occasion, to cover his tracks in the event of an investigation. Never wait more than five minutes: an order no comrade should ever ignore. Punctuality is paramount for militants, they say, it is our backbone and our armor, any delay is conducive to debacle. 7:06. Yahia stays in the car and decides that, this time around, he'd better wait for Fernand. Who knows, a talkative colleague might be holding him up by the machines. 7:11. He gets out, glances around, takes his pack of Gauloises Caporal and lights a cigarette (another one the FLN won't have: Yahia chuckles at the thought of the Front's strictness—bordering on madness—regarding tobacco).

Five more minutes and you're done, dead, bye-bye! Water drips from his nose, he can't breathe. His temples throb so much he imagines them exploding any moment now. An officer, sitting on him, punches him in the stomach. Water squirts out of his mouth. Stop, stop, enough, Fernand can only mumble. The officer straightens up. Another, next to the faucet, turns the water off. Alright, I know where the bomb is . . . Fernand knows nothing of the sort, of course, since Jacqueline took it with her. Rue Boench, a workshop . . . I gave it to a woman, a blonde, yes, that's right, blonde . . . She had a gray skirt and drove a 2CV . . . I don't know her, my bag was too small to fit both in, she took the other one and left . . . A blonde, that's all I know . . . The chief requests the order sent, no time to waste, to all available patrols: scour Algiers with the present description. The cloth blocking his mouth and nose is removed. You see, Iveton, it wasn't that hard. D'you really think we enjoy doing this kind of thing? We just don't want there to be innocent victims because of your shit, that's all. That's our job, Iveton, I would even say our mission—to protect the people. You see: soon as you talk, we leave you alone . . . All of his torturers sound the same, Fernand can't distinguish between their voices anymore: similar timbre, just a lot of noise, goddamn hertz. What Fernand does not know is that the general secretary of police in Algiers, Paul Teitgen, made it explicitly clear, two hours ago, that he forbade anyone from touching the

14

suspect. Teitgen had been deported and tortured by the Germans during the war. He could not understand why the police, his police, that of the France for which he'd fought, the France of the Republic, Voltaire, Hugo, Clemenceau, the France of human rights, of Human Rights (he was never sure when to capitalize), this France, *la France*, would use torture as well. No one here had taken any notice: Teitgen was a gentle soul, a pencil pusher offloaded from the metropolis just three months ago. He had brought his dainty ways along in his little suitcase, you should've seen, duty, probity, righteousness, ethics even— ethics my ass, he knows nothing about this place, nothing at all, do what you have to do with Iveton and I'll cover for you, or so the chief had decided without hesitation. You can't fight a war with principles and boy-scout sermons.

Yahia crushes the butt of his cigarette under his shoe and goes back to his vehicle. Twenty minutes late: it can only mean the worst. He starts the car and runs into an army blockade, about a hundred yards away. Military trucks have closed off the surrounding streets. Papers, please. Yahia is sure of it now: something's happened to Fernand. A second soldier approaches to tell his colleague to let him through, he's not a blonde and this isn't a 2CV, we're not about to start stopping every damn car. Yahia thanks them in a friendly voice (without overdoing it, either) and hurries to Hachelaf's place—if Fernand is tortured, he might end up talking. They have to warn every contact he is liable to give up.

Hélène is in the back of one of the three Tractions Avant. They take her to the police station on rue Carnot, sit her down on a chair in front of a gleaming wooden desk. The chief comes in and asks, without explanation, what color her skirt is. Hélène, who does not understand the point of the question, replies that her skirt is gray. Gray, like the one our suspect is supposed to be wearing! the chief exclaims.

Fernand is still on the bench, tied up, slowly catching his breath. He knows he will be tortured again when they return from the workshop, but he nonetheless takes advantage of the small respite, this unlikely lull in the proceedings. His head is pounding. Torn up. Eyes half closed, he gazes, slack-mouthed, at the ceiling. His genitals hurt especially—so much so that he wonders in what state he'll find his balls when all of this is over. The door opens, he turns his head slightly to the right, hears them yelling, the apes coming in, tricolor-clad Gestapo. A brutal kick twists his lips. You took us for suckers, didn't you, you piece of shit, there was nothing in the workshop . . . we're going to fuck you up good.

Hélène has just been apprised of the situation: her husband has been arrested for planting a bomb, which was immediately defused: the police were called to his factory in Hamma, and found papers on him indicating that another explosive device was supposed to go off— any minute now, in fact. She had no idea, she answers, truthfully. Of course, she is not unaware of Fernand's political views, of his activities in circles of which she knows neither the ins nor the outs, of course she suspects that he could, one day, radicalize further and seek to translate words into action, but she never imagined him capable—is that even the proper term?—of committing, or even wanting to commit, a deadly attack. All she says aloud, however, is that she was entirely ignorant of Fernand's militancy; she loves the man himself and does not care whether his heart beats left or right, as long as it beats by her side. Do you take us for fools, Madame Iveton? She smiles. Her calm is not just a mask, a display of bravado, a protective swagger. Not at all; Hélène has, throughout her life, always known how to maintain the elegance and bearing people expect of her in any situation. You should talk, Madame Iveton, fact is we have a lot of information on your husband, some of which, I'm sorry to say, might hurt you: he's been cheating on you for a while now, with a certain Madame Peschard. Hélène does not believe a word of it. Their speech is heavy and ill-sounding, clumsy, the flimflam of officials and servicemen. She smiles again, before remarking: I hear adultery is fashionable now, I shouldn't be surprised if you, too, chief, were every inch a cuckold.

Fernand has fainted. He had the sensation, right before passing out, that he was about to drown, his lungs filling up completely. An officer slaps his cheeks over and over to bring him round. He's not going to give out on us like that, is he? Teitgen wouldn't be happy. Mr. Ethics. That office clerk from Paris, with the soft heart, all lovey-dovey. They laugh.

Yahia does not find Hachelaf at home, only his wife, who is not aware of anything. He goes to Hachelaf's garage and, after about half an hour, sees him coming up on his Lambretta. He motions for him to stop and explains the situation in a few words. Hachelaf has not had any news from the group, but he was surprised, listening to the radio, not to hear of an explosion at the factory. Yahia offers to hide him for a few days at his European friends', the Duvallets, they're good people, you'll see, and it's only until we find out exactly what's happened to Fernand. He accepts.

Hélène is taken to a cell. Rounded-up prostitutes a few meters away. The water has been cut off.

Fernand comes to. Everything is dim, cops' faces are leaning over his, and his nasal cavity is a violent, searing pain. He wants to vomit. An officer asks the others to stand back and sits on a stool, the very same on which the generator stood only a few hours earlier. He speaks to Fernand in a calm voice. Friendly, even. He has shown courage—it'll be to his credit—but it's useless to keep this up, come clean once and for all and we'll leave you alone, you'll go rest in your cell, no one will hurt you, you have my word. Time's up, you see, we've heard no report of an explosion, your blonde in the 2CV must've found a way to defuse it . . . It's all over, you can tell us the rest, we just want to know who you work with: names, Europeans, Muslims, and don't tell me you don't know anyone. Honestly, I don't know anyone, Fernand affirms it . . . Get back to it, guys.

Prostitutes of every size and shape, varicolored, full-cheeked, plump, bamboo-thin in fishnets, wrinkled or otherwise marked by the smoothness of a desecrated youth. Hélène is sitting at the back of the cell; the cold seeps under her dark green coat. Fernand always said that he condemned blind violence on both moral and political grounds. This arbitrary shredding of bodies, chalking up

18

victims at random—it's a throw of the dice, a sordid lottery on any street, café, bus. Though on the side of the Algerian independentists, he did not approve of their every method: barbarity cannot be beaten by emulation, blood is no answer to blood. Hélène remembers other attacks, that of the Milk Bar and others, and how Fernand worried, telling her over coffee (black, no sugar), his forehead more wrinkled than usual, that it wasn't right to place bombs just anywhere, not right, not at all, to place them among little girls and their mothers, grandmothers and humble Europeans, people without a dime. It could only lead to deadlock. An officer stops in front of the cell and taunts: *Iveton, tête de con!* Hélène stands up. Come say that to my face if you're a man, open up and come say it. The prostitutes clap and let out a few bravos. A baton runs noisily along the bars, demanding immediate silence. Fernand would never have placed a bomb in the factory knowing it would kill workers, of that she is certain. He probably expected the building to be empty. A symbol. Sabotage, in sum.

Let him be, that's enough, or we'll lose him. Fernand is no longer answerable for anything. An unrelenting throbbing inside. Organs like so many wounds. He begs for the water and the blows to stop. It's late, his comrades must know he's been arrested, they've had time to hide. Alright, wait, alright . . . I know two people, no more, I swear, Hachelaf and Fabien, a worker, Italian family, he's young, in his twenties . . . Fernand has no idea who he is talking to and, in truth, knows nothing but the fact that when he talks the torture stops. I don't know anyone else, you have everything. An officer writes the names down in a leather-bound notebook. That'll do for tonight, take him to his cell. He is unable to move by himself: they carry him, naked, to the cell, and toss his clothes nearby. Rats scurry in the corners. Sleep prevails over pain: he collapses a few minutes later.

The River Marne sticks out a green tongue to the sky's peaceful blue.

Clumps of trees unsettle an otherwise rigid horizon.

Fernand is in a short-sleeved shirt and his thin mustache has been freshly trimmed. Up above, the sun oscillates between two wrinkled, if ageless, clouds; down below the grass is speckled with poppies. There are hardly a thousand souls in this village of Annet. Fernand waves at an old fisherman and at someone who must be the fisherman's grandson. The hospital doctor was right: he can feel that, too, he's getting better. The air of the mother country is not without merit. Might he even, before too long, step onto a pitch again and play the soccer he loves so much? Be patient, be patient, said the aforementioned doctor, in a voice calmer than the Marne.

Fernand sings, something he goes in for whenever the walk or the mood demands it . . . *The trees in the night lean in to listen to this sweet song of love* . . . A tango. *Carmen.* The women of Clos-Salembier, his childhood neighborhood, always maintained that he had a nice wee voice, with a certain something in its timbre, a catchy roll, and that he should've tried his luck (they'd go on and on about it) in the cabarets or music-halls of Algiers. *The birds say it again so tenderly . . .*

It must also be acknowledged that the presence of pretty Hélène, whose first name is as lovely to the ear as her namesake, has played a part in his convalescence. She is from Poland, he gathers, overhearing a conversation she had with customers some two weeks ago. Her hair is thick and a distinctive shade of blonde, not unlike hay (slightly dark, matted and rough). Her eyebrows are thin, a pen line at the most; her chin is dimpled and she has prominent cheekbones, the likes of which he has never seen: two promontories above large cheeks. Every evening, or almost (a painful almost, since it marks her absence), Hélène helps her friend Clara, who runs the family *pension* where Fernand is staying, the Café Bleu. She makes appetizers and desserts. During the day, she works at a tannery not far from there, in Lagny—a village, she told him four days ago, that was virtually destroyed during the Great War. The first time Fernand saw her, she was serving wine to a couple seated a few meters away from him. Hélène appeared edgewise, her perfect profile projected on the wall behind her, that shadow slightly swollen, in the middle, by her nose. He noticed her smile, and that cheek—he saw only one at first, obviously—a Mongol's cheek (Fernand has never met any Mongols, but that at least is the image in his mind). And then those eyes: their far-flung blue, journey and meridians for the North African kid he is. Two little tablets, pointed and cold, colored the kind of wolf-dog blue which rummages around your heart, never asking for permission or wiping its feet on the doormat—for this blue would not fail to make a doormat out of you, one day, if it could ever come to blame or love you. He had used indecision as an excuse, at a meal last week (the choice was caramel-cider tartlet or strawberry crème brûlée), to incite their first exchange. She was partial to caramel and asked him where his accent was from: from Algeria, ma'am, it's my first time in France, well, yes, they say Algeria's in France, sure, but still it's not the same, you have to admit that it's . . .

She is here tonight.

Fernand sits down and orders the set meal. Her eyes are little frosted pearls, she smiles and goes off with his order, explicit creases at the back of her skirt, ankles as slender as her wrists . . . Hélène was born in Dolany, a village somewhere in the middle of Poland. Her parents named her Ksiazek at birth, and the family, the three of them and her brother, migrated to France when she was eight months old. For work. They were agricultural laborers. Her father is called Joseph—like the Judean carpenter or the Little Father of the Peoples, the choice is yours—and her mother Sophie. He plays violin and she comes from a wealthy family. She let her class down to escape with the man she chose to love . . . too few hearts are ready to break ranks. They settled in Annet, with chickens, rabbits, four pigs and a few pigeons.

But Fernand does not know any of this yet: he learns it in her car a few days later, when she takes him to the hospital in Lagny for his lung X-ray (he pretended not to

23

know where to go and asked for her help, innocently, this evening, since she is from around here . . .). She has no memories of her native country, Hélène explains while driving her car, and only knows what her parents have told her about it. Her father lives there now, a very unfortunate affair: he only meant to go for a brief stay, but the Polish People's Republic never allowed him to get a return ticket. His letters exude all of his bitterness. Fernand does not hide the fact that he votes with and for his own, the workers. And while he may not have read Marx like the Party leaders, each and every page of *Capital* and the thousands of notes at the bottom of each, he has no doubt that *it* will necessarily happen, one day, the sooner the better: do away with all of that, fat cats, landowners, milords, money-men, scoundrels—those that own the *means of production*, as those leaders like to say. She laughs: why not? Communism would be nice, sure, provided that it's actually implemented, equality for all, the real thing, without bigwigs or bureaucrats, without propaganda or political commissars. But that doesn't really exist anywhere, not even in the USSR, she points out. Fernand won't attempt to deny it: and besides, how could he? His every answer takes the form of a slightly foolish smile. It's right here, we're almost there, she says, pointing to the hospital. She parks and Fernand, at the window, tells her he'll be quick, promise, you can wait for me at the café over there. He takes a bill out of his jacket pocket so she can pay for a beverage, but she refuses, it's useless to insist.

A tough one, this Hélène, thinks Fernand while climbing the steps. A hell of a woman.

One of the two names "given" by Fernand is currently asleep. His bedroom door opens, handguns and automatics at the ready, hands up! Flashlights are pointed at his face. Someone hits the light switch. Fabien gets up, dazed, but he understands full well what is happening. Iveton wishes you a good evening, an officer adds, as if it were not already all too clear. The room is turned upside down and electric wires are found in a cardboard box, under a pair of pants. Fabien takes a punch to the solar plexus. Doubled over, trying to catch his breath, he takes another and falls to the ground. Is that what you make your bombs with? Go to hell, he answers, before a boot hits his ribs.

Hachclaf's wife has also been arrested. They are both taken to the police station, where they act as if they have never met: no, his face doesn't ring a bell, never seen it, sorry. Fabien is undressed: a stick beats the soles of his feet, electrodes are placed on his testicles, while he keeps promising them hell and the devil, imperialist bastards. He is then coated in a strange liquid he is unable to name, ointment, the cops say, guffawing. Man's capacity to laugh is what distinguishes him from other creatures, Rabelais wrote. It's not a pretty sight. They spread it on his "parts," but it hurts just as much in inverted commas: an acidic sensation, burning, gnawing, devouring, he howls. Just talk and the pain will stop. No, he doesn't know where the laboratory is, no more than he knows who makes the bombs. Fabien bites the inside of his cheeks and not a word comes out of his mouth.

Night passes over his slashed body.

Fernand wakes up. Or rather, they wake him. Aching all over, struggling to walk straight. He rubs his nose—a lingering feeling that he is full of water. The press is here, waiting for you, get dressed. The Director of National Security is up, too, and in his suit, while the police chief, a certain Parrat, tries to match him. A dozen journalists and photographers are ranged opposite. Fernand is in cuffs, his hands in front of him. A frenzy of flashes, blinding white spurts. He squints, hair disheveled and greasy, eyes lowered. He is told that his name is on every front page in the Algerian press. *No doubt, his deed done, he would have placed the deadly device in some car, tramway, or shop, where women, children, and innocents would once more have been horribly mutilated,* asserts *La Dépêche quotidienne* . . . Questions gush out, gobs of spit for public opinion, an animal to the slaughterhouse. He answers as he can, without getting into details, trying not to say more than is necessary. His voice quavers, wrecked by hunger and yesterday's torments. No, his cell has nothing to do with the attacks on the Milk Bar and La Cafétéria; no, he is not a murderer but a political activist. His actions were only directed at the factory, at a plant, that's all, not one person was going to perish in the explosion, he had made sure of it personally, checking with the comrades. Everything was planned so as to avoid bloodshed; yes, he is a communist. He answers all the questions, crossing and uncrossing his hands, ill at ease. They inform him that another bomb, on which was written the name "Jacqueline" (his had "Betty," a friend of Taleb's—but the journalists know that, too), was found in a CRS van at dawn, in the center of town: what has he to say about that? I wasn't aware, I don't know anything about that bomb. So, he thinks, Jacqueline found a way to get rid of it. It never exploded: technical failure.

Djilali is bent over his typewriter. He rubs his eyes. His right eyelid twitches nervously. Jacqueline massages his nape with one hand while looking over his shoulder at the pamphlet he is writing: the FLN claims responsibility, without hesitation, for the action conducted by Comrade Fernand Iveton. He is as courageous a patriot as any. The Algeria of tomorrow is his country, one where colonialism will be nothing but a bad memory, a baleful event in the history of the exploitation of man by man. One where Arabs will no longer be made to grovel before others. A sovereign State, independent from France. Jacqueline asks if he plans to send it to the Front for approval—yes, of course, it's a little sensitive at the moment, best to be on the safe side.

Fabien is lying face up, his arms stretched to either side, his lower lip pissing blood. Unable to hold out, he surrendered two names.

Fernand was tortured all day: he gave up three. Of what stuff are heroes made? he asks himself, tied to the bench, head hanging backwards. With what skin, what frame, bones, tendons, nerves, tissues . . . with what flesh, with what soul are they put together? Forgive me, comrades . . . His shoulders are not broad enough to take on the mantle of the prefect of Eure-et-Loir, Jean Moulin, alias Max, who croaked, his head a mass of bruises, on a train to Berlin. He does not have the guts to call on History with a capital H. Forgive me, comrades, I hope at least that you hid well, I held out as long as I could . . .

Today, thirty or so *rebels* were killed by gunfire or bombs in the backcountry.

But still no *war*, no, not that. Power minds its language— its fatigues tailored from satin, its butchery smothered by propriety.

Fernand drinks a little but still gets nothing to eat.

He sleeps.

He is transferred, the next day, to another city. Tortured afresh. This time, an electrified basin of water is placed below him while he is tied to a folding ladder: water is poured into his mouth, if he moves his butt dips in. They want him to give them the bomb-maker's address, that of Abderrahman Taleb, a chemistry student who joined the guerrillas last year. Fernand endures for more than two hours before screaming at them to stop, he will talk, he knows the place, I'll take you there, okay. He is handcuffed and taken aboard a military vehicle. After about forty minutes, sat in the middle of one of three Jeeps, his finger points to a farm. Fernand has never been here before, he knows absolutely nothing about this place, except that it looks like a farm and corroborates the information he gave while being beaten ("the workshop is in a farm outside Algiers"); he is only trying to put a stop to the torture without yielding information necessary to the network's survival. The building's white plaster cuts through the surrounding green. Twenty or so soldiers move, MAT 49 and Thompson M1A1 in hand, toward the front door—they separate into three squads as they inch closer. Meanwhile, Fernand stands a few steps away from the Jeep, with two guards at his side. Their eyes are fastened on the impending assault. A soldier knocks on the door, waits, no answer, he gestures with his hand before moving aside. Three soldiers come from behind him and break the door down. The two guards squint so as not to miss anything. Fernand steals a peek behind him: trees and, farther, a little ravine, it seems from here. Would he have time to reach it? The soldiers enter the farm.

Fernand starts running; he has covered about six meters when the guards spin round and open fire. He hears a series of reports, two, three, and yet to his great surprise he is not falling: he is unhurt and still running! Shouts behind him. The ground drops abruptly. The incline is sudden, but he neither hurtles nor slips: he jumps. Feels his ankle sprain on landing, stumbles, straightens back up. Around him are large rocks, shrubs, rushes and bushes and, a few meters beyond, a watercourse. No time to run or swim, he thinks, he'll get picked off from up there. He rolls under a small bush, a kind of broom, damn, his arms are protruding, he tries to curl upon himself as much as possible, draw in his limbs, but his injuries stop him folding up as tight as he would wish. Soldiers hurtle down the slope, yelling, weapons rattling, leather boots crunching on dry grass. Fernand can't see anything. Some voices grow distant, others seem, or so he fears, to close in. Think he had time to cross the river? For fuck's sake guys I told you to watch him, you really are a bunch of morons, goddamn morons, go get the searchlight, Daniel!

Does fear mark time with its own cadence? Fernand has the impression that he's been under the broom bush for hours. Cramps and tingling in his thighs. No, he is not delirious, night is indeed falling. A soldier talks about bringing a dog. Fernand has trouble hearing now; they are farther away. The ravine is suddenly raked by a great abrasive light. Fuck, he's right there, guys, right there! Fernand can't understand it, he never moved an inch. We want him alive, don't shoot! The boots get closer, hands grab him and pull him up. One of them slaps Fernand. Your handcuffs, fuckhead, you had your arms out, we saw your handcuffs in the searchlight. Smartass. Take him to Algiers.

Fernand protects himself as best he can; they are hitting him on the head and stomach with a sort of wooden handle. You've had your fun haven't you, Iveton, there was nothing in that farm, just a poor peasant family. Are you going to play your little games much longer? We're in no hurry, we're patient and we've got the keys to your hand-cuffs, you're going to lick our boots for as long as we want, you got that right. He is thrown in his cell with an empty stomach, feet and hands bound.

Djilali has received an answer from the Front leaders: they do not wish to publicly claim responsibility for Fernand's failed attack. Jacqueline, sitting on the sofa armrest, can't understand the Front's reaction. The police suspect the communists, so they'll start by arresting PCA and CDL militants willy-nilly; it suits the Front, I guess, blurs the tracks and diverts attention, Djilali says. Did Yacef write the answer? No, I don't think so . . .

Fernand sits on a stool, arms tied together, blood dripping from his nose. A military officer—another or the same, who cares—revolves around him while going through the day's papers. Just the two of them in this room. Did you see, how funny, they almost all misspell your name. Yveton with a Y. Fernand does not find anything particularly "funny" about these mistakes, but is careful not to let on. The soldier surveys the headlines and occasionally reads, loudly, the few lines which interest him most. Here, listen to this, *the French population in Algeria now knows who the monsters are and where they lurk.* They're talking about you, about communists, not very nice, is it . . . Let's see, *Paris-Presse*, you know it? I can say I've never read it, *communist assassin*, ha-ha, your parents will be proud of you, Iveton (he chuckles again at his own joke). Looks like your little friends are a bit jumpy, aren't they, the Party isn't scrambling to praise your actions. Then again, if I was them I wouldn't either, you couldn't even get the bomb to go off, talk about a good man . . . He keeps on circling, soliloquizing, a fish in a square tank, clearly relishing the situation. On his stool, Fernand does not move. A drop of blood has just fallen on the ground,

31

right between his naked feet. *Le Figaro* doesn't seem to like you much. Then again, you're quite the handsome fellow in this picture, here, how d'you like yourself? He shows him the photo, yeah, that little mustache suited you, proof that proles can take good care of themselves, whatever people say. Fernand has stopped listening. He just wishes he would stop going round and round in that maddening way. Answer me when I speak to you. Fernand says nothing. The soldier rolls two or three newspapers in his hand and, without warning, smacks him in the face with them.

Hélène makes a point of not saying goodbye on leaving the office. No need to see me out, she insisted, I know the way. She exits the police headquarters, discovers it's eight p.m., and walks to the taxi stand a little farther off. A Muslim driver invites her into his cab. Rue des Coquelicots, please. That's a pretty name, ma'am, poppies, *coquelicots*. Oh, but perhaps you're not feeling your best, are you, ma'am? I wouldn't wish to seem unbecoming (Hélène notices the word and, without knowing why, finds it almost comical), ma'am, or nosy, God help me, آمـين يـا ربّ, but I know people better than anyone, I do, and you surely know why? I drive them about all day long. I know what everyone is made of, oh yes, yes, ma'am, don't smile, I can see you in the rearview mirror, well, actually, yes, do smile, makes me happy, my name's Farouk, as I was saying: I know all humanity and nothing escapes me, that's what comes from driving a taxi, and I can see at once that you've got a great sadness about you, but you're proud, that's obvious too, with or without the mirror. So why don't you explain

32

why to Farouk, who's not nosy, or maybe just a little . . .
Hélène laughs. Prayer beads hang from his mirror. You
win, you're good, she concedes. I've just come from the
police station, and I've got quite a few worries, in fact. My
husband was arrested, I don't know if you've followed the
news recently, his name is Fernand Iveton, he . . . No! No!
Farouk lets go the wheel for a few seconds and jiggles his
hands. But of course I know Iveton, ma'am! Everyone
knows Iveton in our country, الله يحفظه, this is incredible!
Madame Iveton in person, in my taxi, no one will believe
Farouk! سـبحان الله, he bursts out laughing, rue des
Coquelicots, is that right? Hélène tells him about the hours
she had to spend at the station, and specifies that she was
not mistreated, that no one touched her. She has no news
of her husband, the police refused to give her any and she
has no way of getting in touch with him. No doubt he's
been beaten, yes, it's certain even, and the very idea is
unbearable, she confesses, but she knows he'll be released:
he didn't kill or even injure anyone, the bomb failed to
explode. Any lawyer could get him out of there. Hélène
says goodbye to Farouk, who refuses to take her money, a
refusal which has nothing to do with politeness but much
more with a command: we do not charge the wives of
those who fight for the people, خليه ربنا يخليـك, take care
of yourself ma'am, yes, good night to you too.

The moon yawns, its white breath a veil to the darkness.
A star-formed meshwork—thousands of little keys opening
the night.

Today, seventy-three *rebels* were killed.

A waitress places two menus on the table. Hélène is wearing a light gray dress with a white collar; Fernand, for his part, has taken this opportunity to bring out the only tie in his possession. He had hesitated a little before inviting her to dinner: too soon, perhaps? She had taken the time to go to the hospital with him, so thanking her was the least he could do. Worst comes to worst, he might invoke the famed "Algerian hospitality"—doing so with false naivety, acutely conscious of transforming a bold move into a touching, awkward act—in order to justify such an imprudent, if not impolite, meal. Yet here she is now, in front of him, noticeably more at ease than he is. He could touch her if he reached out, but this very idea is, already, sacrilegious. And is he even thinking of touching her? Bodies are seldom thought of when this thing is born in the belly's depths. This unnamed thing no word can approximate or identify, this *thing* (the most appropriate term, in the end, for those first times out of time). A vague, crazy thing of vapors, fumaroles, ether, routing every attempt at rationality. A thing we know to be soaked in illusions, fineries, gildings and sands of an instant, but which we fasten onto and give it everything headlong, that thing, yes. Fernand looks at her as others might contemplate a statue or a painting: he lacks the linguistic precision to formalize his thoughts, but he looks at the contours and shadows of her skin, the reflections, the more or less visible pores, the hands (it all seems to concentrate on this point—those hands, that gift or slap, that one might hold or that pull away: the hands of a woman loved, or desired, bear the same heartrending charge, the same sacred fever, as the mouth which one day, without warning, will draw near or withhold itself forever), that foreign smile and those eyes that a bad poet would promptly compare to the sea without fearing to offend her (Hélène is not for commonplaces, nor for doggerel).

He doesn't know much about her, but what he knows is ample enough.

No need to ballast a beating heart.

She has a passion for dance, she tells him. She got that from her father, who used to play the violin at village fetes in France (but maybe she told him that already? She apologizes; he relishes it). She even entered competitions, winning a few of them. Waltz, mostly. But, she specifies, Fernand should not think of her father as an arty sage, head in the clouds. No, the man was first and foremost a farm worker. With the hands to prove it, too, unafraid to show their strength at the slightest slip up. She more than once paid the price, from those hands or a black leather belt, when as a child she was not "strict enough" with the farm animals. Fernand listens closely, careful not to interrupt. Hélène dreamed of being an independent and self-reliant woman. But society makes sure a woman doesn't dream of more than her body allows—the community keeps an eye on her belly, her flesh and her future. She had to marry young, at sixteen, leave the family home and turn her back, if only for a time, on this generous but violent father. Fernand asks if she is still angry with him: she simply shakes her head, and apologizes for opening up so indelicately. I don't know what came over me, I'm not used to, well, I, I know you're only here for a short time, I expect that's why. I'm sorry, Fernand, I've only talked about myself, you must be thinking that . . . I won't say anything from now on, I'll just listen to you. I already know my life, I'd rather hear about yours. She smiles. This rice is terribly good, don't you think? Most certainly. Or a little too salty, perhaps?

Fernand makes a point of controlling his diction, not to sound like a North African hick. She insists on knowing more. Her blue eyes grow warmer, sapphire bubbles, bouquets of sky come down from God knows where. Very well. Fernand deliberately takes his time, passes a finger over his mustache, throws back his head a little, and talks about his father, since she was reminiscing about hers. Pascal, a foster child, raised in public care. His last name, Iveton—spelled with an "I," mind you, not a "Y," he adds immediately—comes from them, from the French state. And your mother? From Spain. She had me when she was seventeen, the same year AC Fiorentina was founded. You don't know them? Their shirts have a big red fleur-de-lys on them, still doesn't ring a bell? So it's true about women and soccer . . . I'm teasing you. An Italian club from Florence. In short, I admit there are better ways to make an entrance. My mother's first name was Encarnación, no need to translate, a lovely name, isn't it? Yes, perhaps, in any case it was my mother's. She died when I was two and my father remarried a woman with two kids, sorry, children, from a previous union, as they say. There, we're even, Hélène. We can really kick off now, if you'll allow the expression—was that alright, did you get it this time? She laughs and calls him a hooligan. You'll have to see about that with my mom, maybe hold her to account, he rejoins with a serious face. Hélène freezes, petrified to think she might have blundered; he bursts out laughing, I'm teasing again, sorry, but the face you just made, he chuckles again, then, seeing the waitress, asks if she'd like some coffee.

A week has passed since Fernand was arrested.

He is told, in his cell, that he will be tried in a military court. The trial is in four days. *Attempt to destroy, with an explosive substance, a building that is inhabited or used for habitation.* The officer reads out the charges without looking up. He has fat cheeks and bad skin. Fernand is sitting on an iron bench, his feet still in chains. Articles 434 and 435 of the Penal Code. Risk of incurring maximum penalty. In other words—he specifies, as if it needed to be any clearer—death. Fernand is surprised not to find himself blinking at the sound of the word. Torture must've fried my brain, he thinks. Since yesterday, a nerve has been throbbing continually near the bicep in his right arm. The communist leadership, the other continues, refuses to get involved: the Party hasn't sent a lawyer. They are wary of that troublemaker Iveton: isn't he an anarchist, anyway? Smells like sulfur, like bombs rolled under Tsarist carriages, explosives chucked in parliament or at a barracks, the pennants black and proud, Auguste Vaillant and all the rest of it . . . The officer carefully folds the paper in four before tucking it inside his back pocket. A soldier next to him tells Fernand that out there, every European in Algeria wants him skinned alive. There are pictures of your mug all over Algiers. A traitor, a felon, a white man sold to the fucking arabs.

Hélène looks her boss in the eyes, down to the bottom of his pupils, to the blackest black. She stares him down for so long and so well that he ends up lowering his eyes to his desk, his boss's desk. He raises his head again and adds that he has nothing else to say to her, she can do as she pleases with her afternoon and they'll send her pay for November (or for the days worked, at least, since he doesn't want her to finish the month) as soon as possible. She does not respond and makes a curt exit, taking care, of course, to slam the door. Management, he let her know, does not mean to keep her on as a waitress, given recent events. She passes the Mustapha Hospital but ignores her usual trolley-bus stop—she prefers to walk home, to calm down. The bastards, she thinks, what a bunch of bastards. She'll have to find another job fast, or else, with Fernand in prison, she won't be able to pay the landlord . . . Hélène will wait for the trial to take place, and then comb through the classi-fieds. She worked as a maid when she first arrived in Algiers, at an engineer's, whose pastime of choice was play-ing tennis with his wife. Friendly people. Might they take her on again? You never know.

Fernand is transferred to Barberousse prison in Algiers. French settlers built it some twenty years after their army invaded the country. A handsome building, really, with its uncluttered façades and pointy dome, the sea behind in the distance, cutting the sky with a determined gesture. He is stripped. Fingerprint on the entry register. Cell number assigned, written on a piece of gray cloth—6101. The trial is in two days and Fernand still does not know who will defend him.

Hélène bought the day's papers on her way home. Still walking in, she goes through the articles on the incident and finds a line, one simple line, which instantly arouses her fury: Fernand was apparently wearing *dirty blue overalls* and *a shirt of questionable whiteness*. There it is in black and white, in today's rag. She places her keys on top of the dresser (or throws them, rather), then tears that page off of the periodical. She's always insisted on her husband being clean and tidy, the crease in his pants neat, the collar straight and not yellowed near the neck. She made a fuss whenever he forgot to adjust his belt so the buckle covered the button of his pants (something he had a nasty habit of not doing), and now this journalist has the gall to humiliate them this way, shamelessly, to paint Fernand as unkempt, a slob. No doubt he thinks himself entitled to disparage workers, to jeer at them from the comfort of his chair, that failure, that hack! . . . Hélène is unable to compose herself. She lights a cigarette and takes two drags. A long breath out. Their cat, Titi, is sleeping, a circle of dark fur against the back of a chair, his left paw over his eyes against the light.

Fernand lies on a bunk in his cell, which he shares with two other inmates, both Arabs. He does not know their names (one of them has been keeping up a rhythmic

snoring since Fernand arrived, the other is at the infirmary).
Even here, the system is colonial: Europeans are given two
blankets while natives get one; the former are permitted
two showers and as many shaves per week, while the latter
are allowed one of each. The door opens. A man enters,
preceded by a guard. He introduces himself to Fernand:
Albert Smadja, lawyer. The two shake hands and the guard
leaves. There's nowhere for you to sit, the inmate apologizes. Smadja has brown hair and coarse skin reminiscent
of wet sand; his eyes are half-hidden under their lids. He
is communist and Jewish. Perrin, the chairman of the Bar,
has charged him with Fernand's defense as the court's
appointment. Fernand listens. He knows nothing, or almost
nothing, of what happens behind the scenes. Smadja
prefers to be straight with him: he disapproves of his actions
but will, naturally, do all he can to plead his case, even if
he is only a young lawyer, just starting out. Miming a chop
to his neck with his right hand, Fernand inquires: my
head? The chairman of the Bar, answers the lawyer, thinks
you'll get a prison sentence because you can't be executed
when you haven't killed anyone. And you, what do you
think? Smadja pauses, visibly embarrassed. His silence
rolls into a ball deep inside his throat. To be perfectly frank
with you, Fernand, I was reluctant to work on this case, I'm
only a third-year trainee, I doubt I have the stature for
it . . . The atmosphere is dreadful in Algiers just now, you
know. They all want, precisely, your head. I spoke with the
chairman and this very morning he asked Charles Laînné
to join your team as well. Don't know if you've heard of
him, he's a very good lawyer, sixtyish, a member of Catholic

42

Relief's Social Secretariat. That's just to say that he is always keen to defend, let's say, good causes . . . Fernand asks what Laînné thinks of his case. Smadja finishes wiping the right lens of his glasses with a handkerchief drawn from his breast pocket, and continues: he, too, doubts whether they could take your life for what you've done. We've had a think together about our line for your defense tomorrow—I know, yes, the time frame is awful, people are after your blood, so the authorities don't want to drag things out, I suppose. The member of parliament Soustelle even claimed that you were planning to blow up the whole city . . . Yes, yes, I'm telling you. Smadja rubs the bridge of his nose with his middle finger. Then, looking at Fernand— sat at the edge of his bunk, eyes focused on the floor and shoulders curved slightly inward—he asks him to describe with the utmost precision the abuses committed against him. Fernand raises his face. His eyes are hollow and purplish, his face gaunt, his beard thick. Then he stands up and, without a word, takes off his shirt. Smadja raises his eyebrows. Bruises, scabs, welts. Everywhere.

Hélène places the sweater, jacket, shirt and pants inside a cardboard box. Fernand must look presentable tomorrow at his trial. It is out of the question to give those scribblers another chance to describe him as a scruffy pig. After picking up the scraps of newspaper from the tiled floor, she takes the keys on the dresser and boards the trolleybus to the center of town. She goes to the prison's front desk and demands, by virtue of her status as spouse, to have this package given at once to prisoner Fernand Iveton, cell number 6101. The officer refuses, on the grounds that she hasn't followed the normal procedure and that it's impossible to deliver items to inmates without previously filling out such and such a form, etc. Hélène announces that she will not move an inch until Fernand has received the package in person; the officer is adamant, too, behind his little red mustache. In that case, call the director, I demand to speak to him. The officer hesitates. Hélène stares him down, like she had earlier glared at Monsieur Trémand, her boss, she glares at him until he yields, which he does because he takes the receiver and asks to speak to the prison director. Two CRS men see her to his office. She takes his proffered hand, briskly. The director smiles and bids her sit on one of the three chairs. He is touched by her tenacity, he admits without divesting himself of his smile. I'm not mocking you, I assure you, I'm certain many prisoners would like to know a woman like you. I've been informed of all your calls and letters over the last two days: what tenacity, what stubbornness! Hélène is somewhat baffled by her interlocutor's tone. She sets down the package in front of her and explains that she absolutely (emphasizing each syllable) insists her husband wear clean clothes during his trial. It's the least one could do, the director answers as he takes it. We'll inspect the contents, naturally, as you would expect, but I give you my word that we'll get them to him if they're found in accordance with the regulations. Hélène thanks him. Then senses, once outside, the presence of plainclothes policemen, or perhaps members of the intelligence services, whichever. She glances back, scrutinizing the passersby, convinced that more than one are following her. Is she losing her mind? No, no. She walks on, turns around. A man stops to ask a street vendor for a cigarette: he stopped at the very moment she turned around. She's not dreaming, no, she's not crazy. Hélène yells at him to get lost.

Good night, yes, and above all be strong, Fernand, says Smadja, patting his shoulder awkwardly. The lawyer knocks on the cell door. Three knocks. The guard opens and Fernand nods for the second time at the court appointed attorney.

The X-ray shows *an opaque stain on a lobe of the right lung*. Fernand has no precise idea of what this means, beyond the fact that the statement's length invites the interpretation that what he took for a common cold, caught after a soccer match in Algeria, may be a more serious illness. Very probably tuberculosis. The hospital in Lagny strongly recommended he go to Paris *as soon as possible* to visit another doctor for further examination. Yet Fernand is not particularly worried. By nature he is accustomed, at the great table of existence, to pour his glasses half-full. Happiness for him is tied to the ordinary. He does not claim to be more capable than he is, and displays himself in the evident modesty of crumpled clothes: without noise, without clashes, only with a sort of well-being of which he has no need to be proud.

Hélène has just finished her shift. Her calves are slightly sore after so much walking (there were more customers than usual tonight, for no apparent reason). Fernand is in his room on the Café Bleu's second floor, lying on the

47

counterpane in his underpants, reading *France Football*. Lille OSC has just won the French Cup against FC Nancy. Two goals to one. Fernand knows one of the goalscorers, Jean Vincent—or at least knows of him through the press, and through having watched a few of his matches. He has a likeable mug, that Vincent: high forehead, Sioux nose. Scored in the seventeenth minute. A knock on the door. He gets up, surprised. Who could it be—he looks at his watch—at 10:40 p.m.? He opens, it's Hélène. I hope I'm not disturbing you? Her presence, more than the question it suggests, grips him to the bone: here he is, as if naked, in a stupor. No, no, of course not . . . Come in, please.

She's been on her feet all day, she says, she wanted to sit down a minute before walking home. Fernand can hardly believe his ears. She's not shy, this one, coming up here at such an unreasonable hour: she could have passed any of the people living on this floor, and they would've had a field day just talking about it . . . What are you reading? Ah, soccer again! Fernand demurs: there's *L'Humanité* right there, at the foot of the bed. I don't know if that's much better. She laughs. Then Fernand asks himself if he prefers her laughing, like this, head thrown back to leave her throat exposed, yet not offering it, either: a playful swan, a fair ribbon of spring, with those small white stubs beating their wings and that high-pitched trill, thin and frail (Fernand is getting lost). Or perhaps he prefers her serious, severe, as she often is, the wrinkle between her two eyebrows more pronounced, a delicate furrow, and that tragic look, a Slavic stare straight out of Dostoevsky (or at least that's the image that comes to his mind, again; he gave up on *Crime and Punishment* after the third chapter. He only remembers one sentence, very beautiful really, he had thought to himself: the hero's mother, the one whose name is impossible to remember, had written her son a letter that ended with *I kiss you with a thousand thousand kisses, yours until the grave*—that's lovely, that is, he told himself). Dumb question. There is no need to choose, he loves her both cheerful and serious: two colors of the same future.

Only one bed in the room, not even a stool or a trunk, nothing. Hélène remains standing and Fernand can guess at her embarrassment. Here, he says immediately, to push it away, I didn't tell you: I got a letter from the hospital around noon. They've diagnosed a bit of something inside, a lung playing up. *An opaque stain on a lobe's* what it is— Fernand corrects himself—is what they say. Funny way to put it, *an opaque stain on a lobe*, don't you think? Hélène thinks that he should take it more seriously. Trouble is, I'd have to go to Paris. Trouble? exclaims Hélène, it's only thirty kilometers away, that's nothing! You know I'm not from around here, thirty kilometers is a long way away on the back of a camel. Hélène giggles, you're silly. Fernand begins: I don't want to inconvenience you, Hélène (he likes to utter her first name in front of her, looking straight into her eyes without blinking and with the impression, as foolish as it is fleeting, that he already has her, if only a little . . .), but would you mind if. Hélène cuts in again: don't bother being so polite, stop fussing, I'll drive you there if it helps. Fernand thanks her. Followed by silence.

A passing angel, armed to the teeth. It's late, I've got to go. See you soon, I expect. Fernand nods, he hopes so. And anyway Clara needs help downstairs, we'll cross paths again for sure. He stands up to see her to the door. Cover your neck outside, Hélène, wouldn't want to catch an *opaque stain*, now would you . . .

Paris crumbles under a thick drapery of sky.

The sun shines in little scales, white spittle. Hélène is wearing heels and a striped scarf; her legs are crossed under a round table, outside a café. On the sidewalk, a woman holds a wallet and a baguette in the same hand, a couple hail a taxi (he, a tall twig, sports a blue shirt rolled up to the elbows; she has on beige gloves and a yellow-patterned orange skirt), a man in a raincoat runs across the street without stopping, the policewoman on the square shakes her baton, the metro station on the corner breathes passersby in, out with the same continuous movement . . . Hélène tells Fernand about the war, hers anyway, in which part of her family in Poland was massacred by the Germans. One of her uncles, Sławomir, was tortured for a whole night by a Nazi officer before they finished him off with a saber. Her parents—her father, she specifies, was still in France, he only returned in '48—hid Jews during the Occupation, and she herself fed a friend's brother, a young Resistance fighter in hiding, a member of a network whose name she doesn't know. She never ascertained how it happened, but she was eventually found out: the Vichy authorities wrote to summon her to a police station in Chartres. I think it was a Tuesday, she remembers. She thought it inadvisable to attend, and fled. She was still a Swiss national, thanks to her husband, even though she'd left him before the war, and she took refuge in Lausanne until it was over. The café owner puts a Mouloudji record on the turntable. *I've the ills of the night / Of the night in Paris / When the girls come and go / And at this hour, I just linger* . . . Hélène suddenly stops talking and listens. She really likes this song, she says; Fernand pretends to know it and agrees, a catchy number, yes, I like the chorus, makes me want to dance . . .

He pays the bill and they walk toward Saint-Michel. Fernand spent three days in Paris when he first arrived; he stayed in Pigalle at his grandfather's, a concierge who works in the Grandes-Carrières district, in the 17th arrondissement, and sells *France-Soir* once his day is done, to make a little extra (or bring a bit more bacon home, as he says, though he happens not to like it very much). He had offered to put Fernand up to help him save on hotels. You'll see tonight, the guy's a sweetie, continues Fernand, and I think he's going to like you a lot! The Seine greens to their right, coloring the clouds in one long stroke. They walk by a movie theater and look at the posters: *The Return of Don Camillo, Newlyweds, Circle of Danger, I Confess*—a Hitchcock. Fernand never goes to the movies, practically speaking, but Hélène treats herself sometimes, once a year, when there's a little money left over. The war, you were saying? Yes, her brother, she resumes, enlisted in the Foreign Legion when Germany invaded Poland. Their shadows touch on the asphalt.

~

Oh, you know, it's not that easy over there, whatever they say: even the southern sun forgets to keep up the act sometimes. His grandfather has made a mustard pork roast. The French authorities don't want to listen to Muslim demands. To the "natives," as they say. It's absurd, in addition to being obscene. Going to drive us straight into a wall, believe me, without any turn or anything, nose against brick. Hélène listens closely while cutting her meat. I don't remember the exact date, if you'll forgive me, but what is certain is that the Arabs have been organizing for years to be heard, to win equality for all, between every community at home, in Algeria. But it's like shouting in the desert. Nothing. Zero. We put them behind bars and abolish their parties, dissolved, reduced to silence and then we stand oh so tall, with Culture, Liberty, Civilization, those capital letters, paraded up and down, scrubbed and polished in front of the mirror, the shinier the better . . . Oh, you should see how much they love that stuff. The day France was liberated—I'm speaking of the mainland, of course, I'll say it again: for me Algeria is Algeria, I don't believe in their French department twaddle, that's like parchment, like flint, it's done for, over. Look at Indochina right now. Ho Chi Minh made it very clear when he told them that a new page had to be turned. No one listened, and now look where it's got us . . . Well, so: the day France celebrated victory over the Germans, I don't know how many Muslims, thousands, more, were being massacred in the country, at Sétif, at Guelma. Those names probably don't mean a thing to you, they're about 300 and 500 kilometers from Algiers. Anyway, the stories I've been told, I wouldn't dare repeat them to you, I promise. Especially since we're eating—and besides, grandpa, I've got to tell you: your roast, it's not just delicious, oh no, even to say that would be an insult, it's, it's (Fernand waves his hands), there are no words to describe it. In short, I need to look into other alphabets to describe your roast (his grandfather laughs and looks at Hélène, then Fernand, hell of a guy this one, you'll see, Miss, he's quite a guy). Hélène smiles and wipes the corner of her mouth with a napkin. Fernand hesitates: I'm not boring you with these stories, am I? Oh no, not at all, it's really interesting, on the contrary. Fernand passes a finger over his mustache and resumes: I was born in '26, wasn't even twenty at the time but I remember those things very well, Arabs would tell me about them when we talked. The kind of stories that wreck your sleep. People burned alive with gasoline, crops pillaged, bodies thrown in wells, just like that, grabbed and tossed in, or burned in ovens, kids, women, everyone. The army shooting at everything that moves, to crush dissent. And not just the army, mind you, there were settlers and militiamen as well, hand in glove, all dancing the same damn jig. Death is one thing, but humiliation goes deeper, gets under the skin, it plants little seeds of anger and screws up whole generations; I remember a story someone told me, it happened in Melbou, there's no blood but maybe it's worse, blood dries faster than shame: they forced some Arabs to kneel before our flag and say *We are dogs, Ferhat Abbas is a dog*. Abbas is one of their leaders and still, he's a moderate, wears a tie, doesn't even demand complete

53

independence, he just wants justice. Even the moderates are met with contempt. A French journalist saw it all, I'm not making it up.

About Algeria, Hélène knows only what is reported in the French press. That is, nothing, apart from the state's moralizing piffle. Fernand gets up to help clear the table and make room for the cheese platter. The grandfather begs Hélène to stay seated, it's not every day he has guests, she should make the most of it. How does he see the future? she asks Fernand when they're sitting down again. Fernand's hand goes through his hair. He doesn't really know. However, he has no doubt that things will go from bad to worse. The status quo doesn't work anymore. Some people are talking about the Vietnamese model, to rise up by force of arms and join the guerrillas, but many more, he notes, don't believe in it. Fernand, for his part, aspires to just one thing: that the Algeria of tomorrow end up, voluntarily or otherwise, recognizing all of its children, wherever they're from, him or his parents and grandparents, doesn't matter, Arabs, Berbers, Jews, Italians, Spaniards, Maltese, French, Germans . . . Millions were born in that land, and a handful of property-owners, barons who possess neither laws nor morals, have reigned over the country with the assent and even the backing of successive French governments: we must get rid of this system, clear Algeria of these kinglets and create a new regime with a popular base, made up of Arab and European workers together, humble people, the small and the unassuming of every race united to defeat the crooks who oppress us and hold us to ransom. His grandfather sniggers: here he goes with his communist fancies, don't listen to him Mademoiselle Hélène, when he gets into his stride, the seas start swelling and the levees break!

On the floor like a flattened pigeon, his hair.

The scissors expertly perform their task: Fernand's head is soon bare. It is then tilted to the left, while a razor blade goes over his cheek and shaves a beard which, since his arrest ten days prior, has grown seriously long. Two armed guards are on hand to ensure the operation runs smoothly. Fernand looks at the brown tufts scattered at the feet of the man wielding the blades. It is seven in the morning.

He is presented with a package his wife insisted they give him: clean clothes for his trial. He puts them on. The guards don't even bother to turn their backs. A van awaits downstairs, outside the prison. He gets in, hands shackled behind his back, head bent forward. Not a word has come out of his mouth since he woke up. He distrusts words, now: he knows they can be torn from him by force and turned inside out like a glove. The military court is in rue Cavignac. Journalists and photographers are present en masse and there is much jostling in the crowd. Hélène came with Fernand's father and his second wife. She cut her hair a little shorter last night—or a friendly neighbor cut it for her—without knowing why, just to think about something else, if only for thirty minutes. Pascal, the father, clenches his jaw. He has hardly slept. Grayish eyes, purple swellings. On the way, Hélène told her parents-in-law that they must absolutely not shed tears in public, must avoid the slightest show of weakness or fear. All of them, the press and the public, would love the chance to gloat at their torment.

The doors to the court open and everyone rushes inside. A flock of birds of ill omen. That's Iveton's wife, that's her, they're shouting already. Who could have recognized her? Hélène does not turn around, she lets the calls grow louder, the gobs of spit and hatred roll off her back. She is shoved (too roughly for her to think it was an accident), and elbows out in response, still without turning around. She refuses to turn her head for those who would sever that of her beloved. The small courtroom is packed with curious onlookers. On a balcony, twenty or so armed soldiers. They sit in designated seats. Once the public have taken theirs, seven judges enter, all in military uniform, colonel, captain or second lieutenant. Granjean, Pallier, Longchampt, Nicoleau, Graverian, Valverde and Roynard—the names of those about to judge a traitor.

Two gendarmes take Fernand to the dock. He makes his way with head bowed, cheeks more sunken than usual. It takes a few seconds for Hélène to realize that it is really him. What have they done to him, she asks herself, her stomach immediately twisted, clenched, smothered by grief and anguish. She recalls her own injunctions: never show feeling, never give up. And then she looks at him, her handsome love, with his nearly bald head and vague, vacant eyes. So vacant she cannot call them *his*, since those animal eyes do not reveal the man he is: beaten-down eyes, absent. And his mouth, closed as if condemned to remain so. And that bony face, a corpse's mask on a captive body . . . They've even shaved off his mustache, the scum. Fernand looks for her, his gaze wandering over the audience. He surveys each face, hoping to find the one without whom, he fears, he has nothing left. Hélène's sole presence would allow him to face this squadron of uniformed inquisitors, even if they cannot talk to one another. He finally catches sight of her, flanked by his parents. He smiles: she's cut her hair a bit, he notices. Her blue eyes flicker in the distance, two tiny lanterns in the night of Justice. He sits down. She makes a sign for him to close the top button on his shirt, but he doesn't understand. He frowns, she gestures with her hands. In vain. Journalists wonder: what kind of code is this?

The presiding judge begins by reading the charges before he declares that Fernand may incur *the death penalty*, unless *extenuating circumstances* can be determined and therefore proved. Then he questions Fernand directly. Yes, I am a communist militant. Fernand has raised his head. They look at each other, and he continues, the clerk listening attentively: "I took the decision to become one because I think of myself as Algerian, and I am not indifferent to the struggle of the Algerian people. It seemed to me wrong for the French to stand apart from the struggle. I love France, I love France very much, I love France enormously, but I have no love for colonialists."

Whistles and exclamations in the audience. "Which is why I accepted." The judge asks him if he had planned, within his militant cell, to use *all* means necessary. Fernand answers: "Not all. There are several ways to take action. For our group, it was never a matter of destruction by all possible means, or of making an attempt on anyone's life. We were determined to draw the French government's attention to the growing number of combatants fighting for greater social happiness in this land of Algeria." Yesterday, Fernand prepared statements which he could recite with clarity and precision. He tidied up his thoughts so as not to be taken unawares. He determined to speak calmly, in a warm and serene voice (or so it must sound, at least), without tempering anything of his commitment or the strength of his convictions. He specifies that he chose to place the bomb in a spot he knew was deserted. Hélène looks at him, she sees him in profile, his square face, angular, his beautiful pointed nose. She feels pride, of course, but not just that: an irrepressible desire to take him in her arms and lift him out of this hellhole. His friendship with the traitor Maillot, Henri Maillot, is reported, and the presiding judge asks him whether he knows the damage that his bomb could have caused had it not been discovered in time. "It would've collapsed a partition or two. I would never have accepted, even under pressure, to act in a way that caused death. I am sincere in my political ideals and I believed that my actions would prove that not all European Algerians are anti-Arab, because this gulf keeps on growing . . ." Judge Roynard shrugs and makes a show of his astonishment at the idea of bringing people closer together by fomenting an attack. The laboratory director hands in his report: he explains that, sure enough, such an explosive device can only impact a radius of three to five meters, not enough to demolish a concrete wall. Roynard nonetheless affirms that the bombs of the Milk Bar and La Cafétéria recently provoked a great many innocent fatalities, and that Fernand's undertaking cannot but remind us of those vile deeds. The accused strongly objects and demands to be judged on his own case, not on the actions of others to which he has no link. Oriol, the foreman, comes to the witness box. So it was him after all, the snitch, thinks Fernand. Oriol assures the court that the closet was by no means abandoned, and someone could easily have been there—someone like himself, to begin with, who patrols nearby at 17:45 every day. An engineer corroborates this, also claiming to stop by every day. Fernand interrupts him, almost brutally: "When did you ever have to go there at night?" Unsettled, the engineer replies that no one has ever done that, it's true, in the four years he's worked at the factory. A police officer and his chief follow him into the box. Then Fernand, on his feet, suddenly lifts his shirt, having quietly unbuttoned his jacket during the officer's testimony, and raises his voice to denounce the atrocities committed against his person. "Ten days later, I still bear the marks! They tortured me!" he shouts. The audience simmers, grows agitated. Silence must be called for. His two lawyers, Laînné and Smadja, demand a doctor to examine the accused. The court grants their request—but stipulates the services of a military doctor . . .

61

The hearing is adjourned.

The room empties out, a slow trickle of souls in wait for drops of thick, living blood. Hélène blows a kiss to Fernand from her palm. The two gendarmes who took him to the court now push him into an adjacent room. Fernand sits on a bench. He thinks he spoke as well as he could, he hopes he was convincing. They cannot execute him for a bomb that didn't explode and which, as even the laboratory director agreed, could hardly have harmed a large fly . . . Fernand is not too worried, therefore. France, even if it's a colonial and capitalist republic, is no dictatorship; it will see what's what, be able to disentangle truth from falsehood and read between the enemy's lines. A man enters, he is the doctor. They greet one another, Fernand removes his shirt and the man—thickset, with particularly bushy eyebrows—examines his torso. Neck, stomach, shoulder blades. Fernand mentions that he was also tortured on the rest of his body and, without waiting for a response, unbuttons his pants. Well, well, remarks the doctor, who has from the start avoided meeting the prisoner's eyes. I shall write my report at once so that the judges can read it before the court sits again, at three o'clock. Fernand thanks him.

He is given something to eat, and then the trial resumes. The government commissioner declares that whatever Fernand's intentions—to kill or not to kill innocent people—the crime remains the same. The medical report is read out: the accused has "superficial scars on his torso and his limbs" but, due to their age, "the exact cause of these marks is impossible to ascertain." Fernand asks to

62

speak, permission is refused, and the commissioner continues: in the name of those little children who were sacrificed
in cafés, it is important to punish criminals. Solemn, and
with History ensconced on the tip of his tongue, he
concludes: "You must also think of France, whose prestige
and influence in the world are blemished by these
monstrous acts." The death penalty is therefore, in his
view, required. Smadja protests against the little time—
and that's an understatement, your honors!—the court
lawyers had to prepare their client's defense. The perni-
cious atmosphere, he continues, this cold atmosphere,
drunk on resentment and fury, is not conducive to a proper
review of the case: we must judge Iveton not for attacks
committed by others but for his personal actions, and those
alone. Smadja speaks in a clear, high voice, without
moving his body. It's been shown that the room was abandoned, proved by several witnesses, and it is only fair to
perceive my client's sincerity when he forcefully affirms
that he did not, that he could not, in logistical terms,
mount an attack upon the life of anyone. Laînné endorses
this and, with his bullish body, rams the defense's point
home: "For once, I agree entirely with the prosecution. As
the government commissioner said: 'the prestige of France
hangs in the balance.' France is the land of the rule of law!
The mood surrounding the case assigned to you is heavy,
sorrowful, bereaved by appalling acts which call for the
utmost severity. And yet, precisely because of that, justice
requires that you do not let yourselves run aground on the
shoals that may await you." Rustling in the court. A few
boos. Now Laînné improvises an attack on the Communist

63

Party, which would appear to have manipulated his client, a nice, ingenuous boy, armed only with good intentions. The lawyer knows that this argument, in view of the rabid anti-communism of the authorities and of the court, could advocate for mitigating circumstances. Fernand is surprised by his line of defense. He has never met this Charles Laînné, but Smadja told him that he was known and respected by his peers. No doubt he knows what he's doing . . . And Laînné now calls for the judges' leniency: yes, Iveton must be punished but, in order for this to happen, he must remain alive to atone for his mistakes (when Fernand hears the verb *atone*, he remembers that Smadja also presented him as a devout Christian). All the same, it might be detrimental to imply that he acted under the influence of others; Fernand speaks for the last time and, calmly, explains once again that he could not remain indifferent to the evolution of *his* people, that of the Arabs and Europeans united together. "I had to join in with its action. But never, I repeat, never would I have wished to take part in an action which would have led to someone's death, even if I had been forced to."

The court announces that it will now withdraw in order to deliberate and reach a decision.

His grandfather probably thought they were a couple: just the one bed, no mattress on the floor. Hélène and Fernand make no mention of it but the thought is on their minds. She undoes her hair while he unlaces his shoes. If you want, he says, I can sleep on the floor: it's not that uncomfortable and I've got a good back. I don't know, do as you like, but I'd feel guilty if you were to have a bad night . . . No, don't worry about me, really, I've been through worse. Hélène responds with a smile. She dares not admit that she would prefer to have him by her side, under this coarse blanket—maybe he'd take it amiss? Maybe she's jumping the gun, since he still won't address her informally, with the familiar *tu*? Fernand keeps his sweater on, afraid of seeming too forward. He does however claim one of the bed's two pillows, and then a quilt from the wardrobe. He lies down in it after cushioning the floor with one half. Hélène goes past him, through to the hallway to brush her teeth. The light in the room is turned off. She comes back, slips inside the bed. Good night, Hélène, sleep well. You too.

A broken sun, shining in shards.

Burning the capital with fresh cuts.

They walk along the Canal Saint-Martin, on Quai de Valmy. He has just received his test results from the hospital: *aerobic bacilli present in the organism*—tuberculosis, in other words. His doctor seemed confident, however, reassuring him that his condition was not serious (cough, very slight loss of weight, but no blood-filled expectorations) and that the treatment should deal with it fairly easily, if followed to term. How long will you stay in France? she asks. I don't know yet, maybe a few months, it'll depend on the disease. Do you miss Algeria? Not always, sometimes, he answers. Never when you're here, in any case. She lights the cigarette she had been fiddling with. Fernand's eyes are locked on her wrists. Her long fingers, thin and graceful. Flesh supple and white. A paper cylinder at her lips. The smoke meanders, almost vertically, then spreads out in blue knots. Her tongue remains unseen. Her teeth are bright. She breathes out her second puff through her nose, which is slightly arched in the middle, yes, as he had already noted privately. Her silence embarrasses him. You know, he says as she brings her cigarette to her mouth for the third time, I just thought of something while looking at the birds out there, on that tree. We played this game when I was a kid, a strange game, come to think of it: we'd try to catch sparrows with these sticks, coating them in glue and then chasing the birds or, sometimes, spying on them. We'd wait, gently, slowly, for the right time to bring our sticks close and catch them. Hélène makes a disgusted face. Yes, alright, it wasn't very clever of us. Kids, you know, snot-nosed rascals. Then we'd put them in cages and give them names. Hélène maintains her silence. Something wrong, Hélène? Is it my story that's . . .? No, not at all, don't you worry about it, no, I was just thinking, and I hope you won't be cross, I've kept something from you, or at least I didn't tell you about it, I, I have a son, and, well, he's thirteen, his name is Jean-Claude.

They'd stopped near a canal lock, in front of the Hôtel du Nord. The sky sieving through the leaves. Midges slipping within its folds of light. Green wavelets lapping on a mossy stone, the shapes of yellow snakes. The air is sharp, humid—almost putrid. The water flowing nearby muffles the surrounding sounds and seems suddenly to take them out of the city. They raise their voices. A son, yes. Fernand is more surprised by the secret than by its content. I don't know, she continues, a single woman with a child isn't looked upon too kindly, I think I was afraid you'd judge me like that, it's a bit silly, I know . . . Fernand asks if he can have a drag of her cigarette. He's only smoked three or four times in his whole life. To mark major events. He laughs. She divorced her husband—the Swiss, cuts in Fernand. Yes, Swiss—when Jean-Claude was only eight months old, I know it doesn't improve my case . . . I'd only married him to get away from home, a long way away, but we weren't really suited, we only had the child in common, that's about it. That's not nothing, Fernand says while handing her cigarette back, which she then takes to her lips. He never saw his son grow up, I don't even know if we can call him his father. The separation was, let's say, let's say there was shouting and a saucepan thrown against a door . . . Fernand laughs again. The cigarette is spent. Hélène throws it down on the road, to their right. Fernand peers at her, narrows his eyes and pulls a serious face, exaggeratedly serious, something is bothering me a lot more than this business about a secret child: your cigarette. Sorry? My aerobic bacilli, my nasty little bacilli, they might be contagious, don't you think? If I've just given you tuberculosis, I wouldn't bet on your chances of survival, seeing the size of your wrists. Hélène guffaws. You idiot, you. She called me *tu*, Fernand thinks instantly. They stare at each other, a little foolishly. Let's find a restaurant around here, he suggests, I'm starving!

Hélène leafs through today's *L'Humanité*, lying on her stomach, legs crossed and encased in gray stockings. Fernand is sitting on the edge of the bed, shining his shoes. The bedroom smells of cold tobacco. Four cigarette butts in a cracked porcelain ashtray on the nightstand. Her skirt has horizontal stripes. When he turns his head slightly to the left all he can see of her is her lower back and her legs, bare-footed. Her flat-heeled shoes are by the door, placed neatly side by side, as per their last motion. He has no trouble divining the curve of her buttocks, stretching the pink stripes of the skirt. The firm volume of that skin. Ample, animal. He can discern the seams of her lingerie. An escape track, sacrilegious. She is motionless—her legs form a triangle, a perfect right angle. She turns a page of the newspaper. Is she really reading or pretending to?

Fernand puts down the shoe he was holding and the polish-coated rag, scrubs his hands on a handkerchief pulled from his pants pocket, then turns toward her. Or at least turns his body to sit against the wall, legs spread out before him. What are you reading? Nothing, well, yes, about a coup attempt in the GDR, that's what it says. She sits up and shows him the article, a state of emergency has been declared, counterrevolutionaries in the pay of the West are spreading chaos in East Berlin. I don't know much about it, says Fernand. Propaganda, just like in Poland, all bullshit, says Hélène decisively. Her back is now upright against the bedroom wall. She moves the pillow, for comfort, and unfolds her legs, an absolute insolence of calves and knees, parallel to Fernand's. She is beautiful. Beautiful enough to make you wish you were blind sooner than see her go, disappear, run into another's arms. The circle of her right cheek is fringed by lamplight. Rosette, silken scoop.

He moves his hand slowly and brushes it against her forearm.

She does not move.

She lets him.

The order is given that it is time to be silent. A scent in suspense. His middle finger caresses a little area of skin, inching closer to her wrist. A small peak of bone. Some fine blonde hairs. She moves her face toward his and presses her lips under Fernand's thick mustache. Moist tangle of tongues. His hand goes through her hair, encircling her now with his heavy arms, his large back, his dry torso against hers, this siren from the East. Braid of legs on the rough cotton. His tongue is not done seeking hers, burrowing in her mouth, expecting her saliva. She unbuckles his belt without looking. Jingle-jangle of gray metal. Strokes her hand over the corduroy, presses the phallus she knows to be already blood-swollen. Squeezes again, more firmly. Grasps the whole member under the seams. Asks him if she *may*. This strange question and nothing else. Fernand nods. He realizes, then, that he is shaking. Not a slight oscillation, either, not the kind of vibration that only he could perceive, no: he is really trembling. Hélène unbuttons his pants and tries to lower them; Fernand has no choice but to help her. She takes him into her mouth. So fast he doubts the reality of what he is currently experiencing. Her face comes and goes, or at least what he can see of it, hidden behind the ruffled blonde of her hair. She seems to take the whole measure of the instant while Fernand is torn out of himself. Her tongue runs over its burning length. Then sinks in once again, swallowing, a boa.

He is inside her now.

Cleft warm and drenched. Sublime crevice in the wall of a woman who offers herself. She closes her eyes and breathes hard. Pants, moans. Lying on her back, thighs parted, flattened against him. He is still in his undershirt. Her bare shoulders, her shaken little breasts. A birthmark on one collarbone. He buries his head in her neck, crudely consuming her scent, madness, the madness of that neck, his hips slam harder and harder into the depths of so much beauty.

Not yet five p.m. The judges have returned to the courtroom. President Roynard takes the floor: Fernand Iveton
is hereby sentenced to death. The verdict falls like the
blade that is now promised to him. Fernand lowers his
eyes as, from the four corners of the hall, clamor erupts
among the European Algerians. Cheers and bravos. Intox-
ication, bared teeth. Justice wallows in its triumph. Hélène
tries not to dissolve into tears, biting the inside of her
cheeks, refusing to make a spectacle of their defeat. One
does not throw this kind of meat to dogs. She grips her
mother-in-law's hand to enjoin her to do the same. Palms
smacking together, unanimous rejoicing like a single fat
body. Fernand, for his part, does not feel like crying.
Torture has dried him up—an empty soul, robbed of all
emotion. His lawyers look at him without hiding their
chagrin. The president calls for calm and orders the
public to leave the court with discipline and restraint.
She tries to catch her lover's eye but he keeps his gaze
down, glued to a floor that is now slipping away from

under Hélène's feet. It would be too painful to look at her, he knows it.

Two officers lead him away; he does not turn around.

The crowd disperses and Hélène lets herself be carried along on the edge of it, trying but failing to walk straight. Her legs are shaking, her head is spinning, she leans on the arms of Pascal and his wife. We'll weep at home, she repeats, not here. They wait for about ten minutes on the sidewalk. A few people stare at Iveton's wife. She ignores them. A prisoner transport van with grilled windows passes mere meters from them but does not stop, of course. Hélène and Pascal wave at it in the hope that Fernand will see them, in vain, since he continues, on a bench inside the vehicle, to look down. His lawyers inform him that he has one day to lodge his appeal—as he intends to do.

He is transferred to Barberousse prison, cell no. 1, first division. Alone. He is a CAM. *Condamné à mort*: death row convict. The room is gray, of course, what else could it have been? A straw mattress and a squat toilet. And a strange smell, impossible to define or describe, vaguely pungent and spongy. And yet you can't deny the cell is clean. Humid, and that is probably what gives it its elusive odor, but clean. They left him his clothes. He sits down on the thin mattress. Away now from the shouting and the contorted faces, Fernand begins to grasp his predicament: the authorities intend to execute him. But he hasn't killed anyone. It makes no sense. The powerful are just blowing their horn, that's all, raising their voices to make an example of him. But they'll never go through with it. Impossible. France is hardly some tyrant. Fernand must, at the heart of his being, come to terms with it: he tells himself that he isn't all that worried. His lawyers will succeed in making his case, he can feel it. They will prevail. And who knows, won't fair-minded souls mobilize on the mainland? His hand passes over the hair that is no longer there. Weird feeling, this nearly bare skull. He thinks of Henri. Henri Maillot, his brother. Two years his junior. A brother in childhood and in spirit—and what is blood, anyway? Nothing but the tangible result of chance. He has to stand upright for Henri, since after all his brother stood upright until the very end, until the gendarmes' bullets mowed him down, and he yelled, he, the deserter, *Long live the Communist Party of Algeria!* . . . Fernand and Henri met as children. Their families lived close together in the neighborhood of Clos-Salembier; their mothers were both Spanish Catholics and their fathers communists: their friendship was thus fully deserving of the term fraternal. And yet they were far from alike—in fact, and it was certainly the view of their respective parents, they were symmetrical opposites: one, Fernand, was of medium height, the other was tall and slender; one had strong features, unrefined, whereas the other's were fine and polished; one was mischievous, the other self-effacing; one loved dancing and singing while the other preferred calm and concentration. Henri thought more than he talked; he held others dear without letting them know it. In a way that was by no means entirely conscious, words were a rare commodity for him—no point wasting language on nothing. He always went straight to the nub, trimming excesses, cutting out the extra, eschewing bloat, and running sharp and straight

73

between timeouts, blurs and detours: Henri could express in ten words what Fernand said in so many minutes.

Hélène collapses in the little front courtyard of their house. In floods of tears. Pascal helps her up. She howls, grabbing her father-in-law's white shirt, and he, decorous to a fault, barely dares clasp her against him. He awkwardly pats her shoulder, whispering that it's going to be alright, the lawyers will do something, we're not going to leave our son like that, we'll find a way, that's right, it's going to be fine. Hélène nervously claws her forearms, head buried in Pascal's burly chest. Spasms overcome her. She is shaking, unable to stop. Her mother-in-law takes her hand and tenderly shepherds her indoors. Their neighbor, at the window, did not miss a thing.

Night, behind bars, does not show itself in the best light.

Gray broth with floating lumps of wearied stars.

Hélène hasn't waited to obtain official visiting rights. In the parlor, some fifty people stand in line to speak to their loved ones. Many of them are Arabs. One of these, a young man, recognizes Madame Iveton, the woman in the papers, in the papers! and applause instantly breaks out. Two veiled women salute her with hands raised to the sky. Others urge her to go in front of them, out of the way, out of the way, it's Iveton's wife, بـارك الله فيــك, let her through! Fernand arrives. Handcuffed. Two barriers separate them in the room. A guard is posted a few feet behind him. Hélène is not the sort who has to try in order to look pretty, but she seems even prettier when Fernand realizes that, despite her sunken eyes and drawn face, she has made herself up for him. How are you? I'm fine, fine. Don't worry. I asked them not to leave me alone in the cell, time passes too slowly otherwise, it's hell being alone between four walls from morning to night . . . They were kind enough to listen, two guys joined me just now, called Bakri and Chikhi, I don't know why they're at Barberousse but anyway, they seem like nice guys. And how are you, then? I hear you're a tigress! He laughs. Doesn't surprise me . . . I'm proud, you know, very proud of my little Hélène. The guard, hearing him lower his voice, curtly asks him to speak up. I promise, I'm going to do all I can to be allowed to visit you every week: I think the prison direc- tor respects me, he received me in his office, you know, for the clothes, yes, the press was saying that you were dirty and shabby, what a bunch of bastards, forgive me for talk- ing like that . . . Speaking of that, what are today's papers saying? Everyone's talking about the sentence. And in France? Your *Huma* is being extremely cautious, it looks like they're reluctant to jump one way or the other. You're an embarrassment. A few lines inside, that's all. And *Le Monde* devoted a few sentences . . . *The terrorist Fernand Iveton*, etc. He says nothing. He longs to touch her, her face or her hands, but the skin of his beloved is striped with iron. Visiting time is over, announces the guard. She tells him she loves him, tells him again and blows him a kiss through barred hands.

The cell door opens while he is chatting with Bakri. A man in a dark suit comes in, escorted by two guards. Receding hairline, long face, glassy eyes. The door closes. He holds out his hand to Fernand: Joë Nordmann, then greets Fernand's cellmates with a nod. I've just arrived in

75

Algiers, the CGT sent me to plead your cause, because, they said, you were one of their union delegates. I've been tasked with assisting the two lawyers already handling your case. I admit I'm not familiar with the details of the brief yet, but you should know that I didn't hesitate for a moment when I was told about your case. Fernand listens, silent. The atmosphere out there is appalling, I imagine you've had wind of it. It stinks of pogrom, if you'll pardon the expression. Everyone wants your head. The appeal, he continues without moving, will be examined next Monday by the military tribunal. Bakri, sitting on the edge of his bunk, asks the lawyer what will happen to Fernand if it fails. Nordmann turns toward the prisoner and, with the oratorical ease which is apparently his forte, responds that from that moment on, one single, final resort remains: a presidential pardon from René Coty himself. Silence in the cell. Fernand asks if he's met his two lawyers, Laînné and Smadja. Not yet, no, we're meeting this afternoon. Trust us, we'll do everything in our power to get you out of here. Everything is still possible, and besides, let me say that I have a personal stake in this affair: I am a communist, too. His face remains perfectly still as he says this; the lawyer knows full well that the very word is laden with immediate complicity.

Harangues of a muezzin, while the night descends and spoils itself on Barberousse.

Bakri and Chikhi pray on the floor, kneeling on sheets specially folded for the occasion. Fernand watches them from his mattress, skimming the newspaper Nordmann left him before leaving. Then he puts it down and takes the few sheets of paper he managed to obtain from management. *My darling little wife . . .* His fellow inmates get up and return to their mattresses. *Today, I'm writing my first letter to you as a prisoner and I don't think this should affect you too much, because I don't want it to. So, today I received my first supplies from the canteen. There's one here where we can get everything the regulations permit, since I don't have the right to an allowance. But still, it's alright; the food is passable and with the little money I still had on me I could spoil myself. As you can see, my morale is good and I think it should be the same for the whole family.* Bakri and Chikhi, he specifies, will soon be released: they're not CAMs. *I go outside in the yard twice a day for an hour, except when it's raining. I hope you were able to fetch my clothes from the factory and that they didn't give you too much trouble. Darling little wife, I am very proud of your courage and my only wish is for you to stay very calm and not fall for provocations, that would be painful to me. And if it's not asking too much, I'd also like you to send me a small money order for the canteen. Finally, I do believe the neighbors are not so nasty; if they say anything, greet them from me and tell them I'm holding up fine.* Chikhi seems to be playing solitaire, cards spread out before him. He is a tall, bony figure, with a falcon's profile. He has barely said a word since arriving. Chikhi is involuntarily mysterious: he doesn't cultivate secrecy, he only shows very little. His manner is not a form of reticence, let alone shyness, but rather a visceral hermeticism—an instinct for concealment, the mistrust of the hunted prey. *I will conclude this letter by kissing you with all my heart and telling you to be*

77

strong and we'll meet soon. Kiss my parents for me and be sure to tell them to keep strong as well. Fernand.

The moon: not yet a crescent, a silver eyelash on a black screen.

And Henri, somewhere beneath this earth. Six months without you, my brother.

A noiseless wind blows through Annet.

The Marne dallies between two tints. Three old oak trees shade Hélène's family home—the home of her mother Sophie. Red tiles and ancient bricks. A farmyard alive with chickens, rabbits, pigeons, and pigs. Fernand greets Louisette, Hélène's sister, then her son Jean-Claude, with a firm handshake. He is tall, taller than Fernand, and wears a beige short-sleeved shirt. Thick chestnut mop of hair. The nose keen and the lips thin. He doesn't have his mother's cheeks, thinks Fernand right away, nor her Slavic features. Hélène invited him to spend the weekend, a fortnight after their return from Paris. She knew it would make their relationship official, recent as it was; she knew above all that this gesture could prove meaningful to Jean-Claude, whom she had kept well away from the few men she had seen since her divorce. Sometimes for fleeting romances; often for casual flings. But this time, though without being able to explain it (not even to herself, probably), she sensed that Fernand would not be just another of those men. She hadn't yet dared confess it to him, but she felt sure that she was falling in love.

Fernand came with two bottles of white wine and a bouquet of lilies. Don't talk right away about being a communist, will you? Seeing what's happening to my dad over there, it might cast a chill. He had promised, of course, before kissing her a few meters from the gate. Jean-Claude understood at once that this man with the peculiar accent, with his mustache and olive skin, was more than a friend in his mother's eyes. He had never seen her look at someone that way, with such a sparkle, such a smile. *Maman*, pipes Hélène from the living room while Louisette is setting the table, Fernand is as big an eater as Jeannot, you'll see, a real ogre! Sophie, wrapped in her apron, wants to know whether he eats all kinds of food. I do, ma'am, absolutely. And I have to tell you that I'm crazy about French cuisine.

He feels at ease, already, in this family that is not his own—hopefulness adds a "yet" to this sentence: it may be his, one day. Hélène appears more tentative, less willful than usual. She is not just a woman here, but a daughter, a mother, a sister; no longer a beautiful atom fallen from the sky, her roots are revealed. Fernand now knows that he will have to love her with others. Love her with those whom she herself loves.

At the table, Sophie questions him on his youth and his childhood neighborhood. A child like every other, ma'am, who kicked balls about with his pals and got into fights when the grown-ups weren't looking. Played marbles with apricot stones, for want of the real thing, and broke streetlights with slingshots. He grew up, he says, in an Arab Muslim neighborhood where few Europeans lived. Almost a village life, where going to Algiers, though not far away as the crow flies, seemed to us like an adventure. It was his father, Pascal, always in blue overalls and a cap—always—who built their house. Saturdays and Sundays, everyone would roll up their sleeves to help out; Fernand was in charge of the mortar. Everyone lived together, the Arab market, the Moorish bath, Europeans and Jews, doors open during the night, women in white veils, you've probably seen them on postcards, I guess, marriages and circumcisions where the whole neighborhood was invited, yes, it was all pretty good, and it still is, by the way. Fernand loved growing up there: we weren't rolling in money, that's for sure, but we made do. And then the sun, ma'am, it's really something to know that it's always there, that it almost never sulks. Call me Sophie, please. It's quite something, Sophie, over there, the sky and the sea. It's like one huge body, all naked and blue. So yes, when you've grown up like that, I can tell you that it's very tough watching your country refuse to move forward, seeing the people in power close their eyes to what's happening, to the small hardships and the great ones, to the Arabs asking for equality and receiving beatings or bullets in return. Sophie marks a pause, then asks if he is a communist. Fernand lowers his eyes then glances at Hélène, why do you ask that, Sophie? Oh, nothing, it's just that I once heard a communist talk like you, so I just thought that . . . My father was a communist. He worked at Gaz d'Algérie and went on strike during the war, so Vichy kicked him out, just like that, buzz off. That's why I left school early. I hope you don't think me too dumb, big oaf in front of all your books in the living room . . . Sophie smiles and admits that she likes novels, that she devours them whenever work leaves her a bit of free time, but all the same they're simple folk, without pretensions (Fernand then remembers a conversation he had with Hélène, who told him that her mother, from a well-to-do family, broke with her milieu to follow her working-class father). That's why I didn't go on studying, I had to help out at home since my dad was fired. That's how I became a turner. The mother's face darkened, she is sincerely affected by her guest's tale. Fernand notices and shouts with laughter: don't make that face, it's not *Les Misérables*, either! And since I never knew my mother, I got to be looked after by every woman in the neighborhood!

Fernand takes advantage of the daily yard break to stretch his legs. He rereads Hélène's letter, which he received this morning. She is trying her best to keep calm, but cannot stand the wait. René Coty, she tells him, pardoned sixteen *terrorists* sentenced to death in the last five months—we must hold on to that, even if the appeal fails. She knows the mail is read and censored and she expresses herself accordingly. Life without him is unlivable. She loves him, yes, how she loves him.

The three inmates have managed to obtain a checkers set. They now devote some of their time to it—that which usage would label "free," between meals and walks, washing and reading. Today is Tuesday. Tuesday, December 4, and Fernand can only think of his lawyers, who yesterday pleaded his case before the court and whom he hasn't heard from since. Time passes and carries away with it his early optimism (if that's the right word when his head is in jeopardy). He now doubts the judges will respond favorably to his appeal. But *I'm confident*, he writes Hélène, *and ready to wait for my pardon. There are some here who've been waiting almost two years, so that cheers me up.* He hugs her close to his heart and asks her to take good care of Titi. This reminds him of his surprise, the first few months, at his attachment to that little bundle of mute fur. Animals had not been part of his everyday life before, and therefore not part of his existence: they occupied silent zones on the margins of the human world, places he had no wish to visit. The thought of hurting them would have never crossed his mind, but he knew nothing about them and had no wish to rectify that situation. Titi was soon following him everywhere, even to the bathroom, jumping onto his lap or the back of his neck, sleeping on his clothes or amid the scattered notebooks on the nightstand. Titi, he remembers with a grin, used to meow in the long mornings when Fernand and Hélène allowed themselves an extra few hours in bed. Titi, Hélène liked to say, was a cat who thought he was a dog: he had masses of affection to give.

Wednesday. What are Smadja and Laînné doing? Why haven't they come? And what about Nordmann?

Thursday. Bakri has gone to the infirmary and Chikhi plays solitaire, without a word, true to himself. Fernand is cutting his nails when the door opens. Nordmann. His face tells him all he needs to know. This time he does not remain standing, frozen in his task, but asks to sit on the edge (but only the edge) of his client's bunk. You know, he says without mentioning the appeal's failure (words can be so cumbersome), I was in Paris in March '41 after my release, after the Armistice. There were German uniforms

84

everywhere, German flags on every façade. I was disbarred because I was Jewish, and went underground, got a new identity as a pharmacy assistant. I became Jean . . . I had to make sure never to write down names, addresses, or telephone numbers. Chikhi has stopped playing; he is listening. I moved about twelve times during those three years. You're probably wondering why I'm telling you all this, aren't you? Within our organization, we were in contact with the families and loved ones of Resistance fighters who'd gone before the firing squad. We published their letters in our bulletins. And this morning I remembered a letter from one of them, his name was René, I think, yes, René, that's it, he was head of the Building Federation, I remember he wrote that he was dying so that the sun might shine on *all the peoples who aspire to liberty*. I remember his exact words. And I was thinking of him, and of you, as I came here. History is cruel . . . With these words he gets up and takes a newspaper from his bag. *L'Huma*, here you are. Fernand thanks him and takes it. It mentions you. He leafs through. Comes upon his photograph. *Iveton—whose life is in danger—courageously expressed the Algerian Communist Party's position before his judges* . . . Nordmann continues: I'll write to the prime minister and try to contact the minister of justice, François Mitterrand. I promise we'll do everything we can to get you out of here. Fernand thanks him, and Nordmann, a quick smile creasing his face as he stops before the door (on which he has just knocked, and which the guard outside immediately opens), declares that Algeria will one day be free and independent, there's no doubt about that.

And meanwhile he asks him not to be so formal and to address him as *tu*.

Fernand tosses and turns in hope of finding a position that would help him fall asleep, but slumber only cares for its own moods. He tries to focus on his breathing—a technique Hélène taught him, convinced of its effectiveness despite her companion's obvious bewilderment—to empty his mind and concentrate solely on the comings and goings of his breath, inhaling, exhaling, thinking of nothing but this rhythmic respiration. But at the bottom of his lungs are the cheers he heard at his trial, along with the faraway features of Hélène, her aroma he could recognize, of course, among a thousand others, though it's so hard for him now to conjure up, to grasp, to seize in both hands. And his father's worries, no doubt, even if one doesn't talk about those things. And his friends, his comrades, of whom he has no news. He fears he was too weak, that he put them in danger—he spilled more than the others probably would have . . . He even catches himself weeping, albeit without a sound: only tears, carving his cheeks as in the distance the night carves the roofs of Algiers.

Hélène is dusting the furniture while the cat snakes between her legs. A knock on the door—the time, which she checks by the clock near the dresser, means it's the mailman. She lays the duster down on a corner of the table and opens the door, after rubbing her hands on the side of her pants. The employee has already extracted today's mail from his satchel. Four letters. Including one from Fernand. Thank you, and good day to you as well, *I think I gather that your spirits are very low and that you have no hope left.*

As for me, I want to tell you that I'm not dead yet and that I hope to end my days as an old man next to my dear Hélène who I love with all my heart. See, I'm the prisoner and yet I'm the one giving you hope for the future. So I beg you, take heart like you've done until now and trust in the future because there's not long to wait, and above all don't be by yourself. Hélène has sat down to finish reading. *And that naughty little cat, what's become of him? You must tell me about him because I'm also thinking of him, I see him in my arms while I read the paper. You must buy yourself some shoes and whatever else you need. I did my laundry today. I received the canteen order: ½ pound of sugar, a jar of jam, a small packet of tousts, two tubes of condensed milk, a quarter of butter and cigarettes. Thank you for the order. I am going to buy a pair of slippers for 650 francs next week. Obviously it's more expensive than in town but there's no other way. You see, my morale is good and you have to be like me.* She thinks of her son, who returned to France after Henri's death. A wise decision, most definitely, but which sometimes weighs on her: his absence, especially in these bitter times, makes her problems feel heavier. Yet Algeria is no place for an adolescent anymore. He belongs in France. At least there's no blood flowing down the Marne . . . *Your husband who loves you and is thinking about you for life.* There is another letter, anonymous, like two or three she others received in recent days. *Sister, you can go where you please, you are protected. Destroy this letter.* No name, but Hélène does not doubt for a second that it came from an Algerian. Like the previous ones. This spontaneous support moves, surprises, and encourages her.

Yesterday, a Muslim man, probably deemed a traitor by the FLN, was gunned down a few steps from their home.

Fernand, Chikhi and Bakri, escorted by three guards, go through a long corridor, then down a flight of stairs. For reasons unknown, an order was given to move them to another cell. From no. 1 to no. 22. Three mattresses, nothing between them and the floor. A lightbulb on the ceiling—pallid when lit, as it should be. At a glance, the room measures no more than six square meters. In the corner, at the back, lies the same squat toilet equipped with a rusty faucet. An old wooden shelf, still holding up, miraculously. Bakri jokes right away: we've had a look around the premises, my word, it's a real palace! Fernand smiles. What if you taught me to speak Arabic, eh, guys? You really want to? And why not? Not sure it'll be any use to me up there, if they do end up chopping my head off—then again, doesn't Allah speak Arabic? Bakri laughs, I'm sure he speaks French as well, with the same accent as you! But yes, with pleasure, what do you say, Chikhi? Chikhi never says much, as we have noted, but he approves nonetheless with a slight nod.

Someone knocks on the door—an indefinite pronoun replaced by Smadja as the ponderous slab of iron screeches open. How are you doing, Fernand? I'm doing, sir, I'm doing. These fellows are helping me through it. We spend our days playing checkers, actually—and yourself, chess, isn't it? Smadja does not catch the pun on *échecs*, which means both chess and failure. War is raging in the interior, he announces brusquely. News is scarce, but I hear from reliable sources that people are getting summarily shot here and there. Smadja scratches behind his ear. He goes on: Friday, *France-Soir* published a photo of your supposed accomplice, the blonde woman, claiming she'd been identified. Fernand doesn't say anything but thinks no less of it: amused, somewhat, that the police have kept chasing this false lead, and reassured by the thought that Jacqueline is safe and sound. We've also been told that the former director of your factory wrote to René Coty—yes indeed, on his own initiative—to ask for your pardon. We've been unable to get a copy of his letter, of course, but it apparently praised your professionalism. And when, asks Fernand, are you going to send in our appeal for a pardon? Soon, but we're holding back a bit, hoping perhaps a movement will develop in the metropolis, something to set off, rouse, stir up popular opinion or, at least, inform it of your predicament. If enough people get behind your case the authorities will have no choice but to concede. A balance of power must be established, pressure applied. Problem is, he adds, and stops. Problem? echoes Fernand. Problem is, continues Smadja, the communists are divided—and that's an understatement—on your actions . . . It's going to be very difficult to rally them all behind you, to launch a unanimous campaign. What's more the appeal process is itself rather unwieldy: we have to complete three dossiers of application, one for the High Judicial Council, another for the Office of the President of the Republic, and a third for the Ministry of Defense. Fernand makes an involuntary grimace of surprise. All that for him . . . And are you at all hopeful, sir? he ventures. Smadja scratches the back of his ear again.

٠١٢٣٤٥٦٧٨٩١٠

Fernand reads and rereads the ten numbers Bakri has written in one of the three notebooks he ordered (twenty-five francs apiece). And then their equivalents in Latin script, to practice the pronunciation: *Sifr, Wahid, Ithman, Thalaatha, Arbaâ, Khamsa, Sitta, Sabaâ, Thamaniya, Tisaâ, Aâshara*. Not bad, says Bakri. But same as every white person, you can't do the "h." You're just blowing, you are, you sound like a tired old mare! Has to come from the back of the throat, like this, *h*, clench your stomach, *h*. Fernand tries and Chikhi laughs: sounds like you're burping on us, now. Don't make fun, guys, there's no equivalent of your thing in French, we can't do it with our mouths, I tell you. And how do you think we do it? Or maybe we don't have the same esophagus? From the top, go on, we're all ears.

Do you know how long we've known each other, today? Hélène stops walking. She thinks, counts on her fingers in their cheap leather gloves, yes, of course, silly me, six months! Yup, continues Fernand, six months to the day since the first time we spoke. It's gone by so fast, is all she says, her eyes on the ground, her cheeks reddened slightly by the frigid air. The path on the right is stifled by large, dry tree trunks. Their branches split and crack the sky— an unbuttressed, defenseless sky, a soft belly sodden with winter. Farther away, mist negates the horizon. Fernand has no desire to spend the rest of the season in France. He misses the North African climate terribly. Look here, I've been meaning to tell you, I've been thinking: I'm going back home. A straight hook to the face. While she's been expecting some such announcement, she hasn't dreaded any less the moment of hearing it. She's seen how Fernand grumbles, a little more every day, about the "lousy" northern weather: drizzle, hail, and even, since the start of the week, a few flakes of snow, immediately churned into a feeble mud clogging their miserable mornings. Especially since the treatment appeared to take effect, or, at least, since he stopped coughing. For Fernand to expose himself to too much cold weather was reckless, anyhow. I understand, says Hélène, you must return home, well, yes, it had to happen someday. I didn't dare talk to you about it but I knew it was hanging, in a way, somewhere over our heads, I knew it would have to . . . Fernand bursts out laughing. Why, what's so funny? My, what a talent for acting, it's like you're on a stage, about to make the whole theater cry! Hélène jabs him with her elbow. Stop it, I don't find this funny at all, you're being unkind now. Not at all, Fernand retorts, I'm taking you with me. How do you mean? What for? Well, for us to get married! I can't marry here, he continues, I'm on sick leave. Hélène had come to expect anything, if not what is best referred to as *that*. But, but, I'm Swiss, I can't get married just like that, with a wave of a wand. It doesn't matter, we'll wait! cries Fernand, a wine-red scarf tied around his neck. But you know very well I'm not alone, there's Jean-Claude . . . I know, I've prepared everything— what did you think? Whatever happens he has to finish the school year, that's important: I'll go back to look for a place to live, and as soon as I find one I'll write and get you both a plane ticket. Hélène does not know whether to kiss him or to slap him, bite his lips or run away, for having allowed her to endure so many—or too many, the two are alike—days in anxious expectation of their breakup. I love you, you great beautiful lady, he says while drawing her closer to kiss the hair on the very top of her head. And I can't wait to introduce you to Henri, you know! We grew up together. Everyone thinks he's a cold fish but take no notice, Henri is a lighter stuck in an ice cube, you just gotta find the wheel!

With his thumb, Jean-Claude slits open the letter his grandmother gave him. *However proud I am of you, as I knew I would be, I am not pleased with you. It's not by banging your head against the wall or crying that you'll ever become a real little man. Also, let me tell you this: you've lived with me and you know what it means to be a communist. Our struggle is hard but we will win. I am not the only man on death row.* The adolescent is angry with his mother for revealing to Fernand that he had cried, but the joy of hearing from his stepfather prevails over this reproach. *Of course, I sometimes cry to think about your mother and all those on the outside, but I have the right, young man, and you don't. So write to me, that I may see your courage, your work, what your friends are saying.* He's never forgotten what Fernand promised him, when he left Algeria two years after joining his mother there: that he was entirely free to think whatever he wanted to think; that he in no way had to share Fernand's political views. Jean-Claude didn't know the whole story (his mother had only told him that his stepfather wanted *equality for all*, admittedly a rather abstract notion for an adolescent) but he could appreciate the most important point: an adult had allowed him to voice his disagreement. That day, he told himself his mother's lover was a good man (Fernand liked to tell Jean-Claude that his mother was his wife from Monday to Friday and his girlfriend on weekends— he would only understand what this remark meant much later: on weekends, factory toil and housework finished, they could love each other more gaily, with the unconstrained and carefree bliss they'd known in France when they first met).

Condensed milk and two packets of cigarettes on a cell shelf. The magazine *Bonne soirée* is open on Chikhi's bunk. Say, brother, says Bakri as he picks his teeth with a thin piece of wood, we were wondering yesterday, during our walk, I hope you won't be angry, it's a little personal . . . Fernand, lying on his mattress, puts down the notebook in which he keeps his penitentiary accounts (a little more than a thousand francs spent at the canteen, November 30, close to two thousand, December 9). Yes, so tell me: you're married, right? Yes, of course, why? So why aren't you wearing a ring, did the prison take it? Fernand laughs, no, you're wrong, way off. My wife Hélène actually forbids me from wearing one: a friend of hers had his fingers sliced off—three, I think, I never met the man—by a machine at work because his ring got stuck. And since I work, or used to, at the factory, she was adamant: no ring! Bakri cannot believe it. My goodness, she thinks of everything, your wife. Hear that, Chikhi? The man in question nods with the tip of his sparrow-hawk nose, smiling along. There were funny moments, says Fernand: one time, we were at a dance party and this girl comes up to me where I'm sitting next to Hélène. After checking out my hand, she suggests we spend an evening on the beach. What did your wife say? asks Bakri. Her, nothing, but me, I said I couldn't, I was married. And the girl looked at my hand again, she must've thought she was doing it discreetly, but in fact she wasn't at all, and asked where my wife was. She's here, right beside you, I answered. And Hélène found it hilarious. Bakri claps his hands while rocking backwards, with all due respect, brother, your wife she sounds even crazier than you!

Fernand drew a hammer and sickle in one of his notebooks and wrote *Prisoner no. 6101's notebook—property of Fernand Iveton, sentenced to death on 11-24-56. Pardoned on . . .* In another, he wrote out from memory the lyrics to those songs he used to hum, when he was outside. This helped him pass the time and, with a few of these light verses, think of something else than that damned heavy ellipsis: *Pardoned on . . .* He knows "Kalou" by Yvette Giraud in full, and sang it one evening, two days ago perhaps—or yesterday, time loses its bearings when trapped in cement—to his two cellmates. *Don't laugh, my fine love is not a game / Kalou, Kalou / In my heart jealousy burns its flame / Kalou, Kalou / My desire no longer finds a happy echo in you / I believe neither your kisses, nor your promises / And yet you do with me what you please / All the time / Kalou, Kalou / Here I am like a slave at your feet / In my flesh you've left a mark so deep / And my soul has suffered so*

/ *With you I'd be happy in Hell below* / *I am weak but I've* *kept enough love* / *To one day open my heart* / *To your* *return, and my delight* . . . Bakri had clapped again, my God that's romantic, brother, is that how you charmed your wife? And Chikhi, in a surprisingly beautiful voice, Fernand thought at once—as if, a strange idea after all, the voice he possessed should bear any relation to the face that housed it (a face that was, truth to tell, remarkably unsightly)—sang a traditional Kabyle air. A warm voice, grave and low. With a little something of infinite tragedy.

The prison chaplain introduces himself, after entering, as Jules Declercq. In his fifties but aging well—firm shoulders, bristly beard. Beneath his clothes can be discerned stout limbs and staunch bones. His hands, particularly hairy, make him look more like a lumberjack than a priest. Fernand is taken aback by his visit. The chaplain explains that he was intrigued by the presence within these walls of a European reputed to be in the anteroom of death (Declercq says this breezily, as if it were simply a status, a vulgar administrative detail). The days are long here, with or without the Lord, and Fernand, on reflection, accepts his interlocutor's disinterested proposition: to talk just for the sake of it. For the sole pleasure of exchanging words. Declercq returns three times during the week, the same smile stretched under his boxer's nose. The chaplain used to be a rural priest: he knows the land and its hardships, its remote corners, forgotten, far from cities and the Progress these embody; he has seen with his own eyes what Camus had written after having seen it, too, in his report for *Alger* *républicain*, the ferocious inequalities in education and wages . . . Not until his fourth visit does Declercq confide to Fernand that he has, in his heart, taken the side of Algerian independence. But he must, in view of his public role, be careful about uttering his most private feelings. Fernand admits for his part that he is concerned about Hélène: how is she managing without her husband's earnings, since she was sacked? He knows, from her letters, that she is selling a number of belongings but fears she may be hiding, so as not to worry him, the full extent of her predicament. Declercq promises to go to their home and find out.

Joë Nordmann comes in a few hours later, brimming with news: the Secretariat of the National Federation of Electric, Nuclear and Gas Industries summoned its union leaders to overwhelm René Coty with telegrams and petitions demanding Iveton's immediate pardon. Parisians, along with gas workers from Aubervilliers, dropped two petitions off at the Elysée; a section of the CGT sent a telegram to Coty. What about our press? asks Fernand. The lawyer's smile fades: nothing . . . Well, yes, the *Huma* is still talking about you. They call for your freedom, but in the inside pages. It's not taking off . . . what a load of shit. This is the first time Fernand has heard his lawyer curse. Don't worry, Joë, everything's going to turn out well, Coty will pardon me, I'm sure: I didn't loosen a single screw, didn't knock a single tile down: how could they cut my head off for that? I know nothing about the law but this doesn't stand up. Nordmann agrees wholeheartedly. Yes, in legal terms, your case is easy to defend, but it's come at the wrong time. War and law have never had a very

functional relationship, the state of emergency, they say . . .
In any case, I managed to get a meeting with Mitterrand's
technical counsel and the director of Criminal Affairs and
Pardons. And how's it going with Smadja and Laînné? asks
Fernand. I'm not quite sure, to tell you the truth, I sometimes get the impression that they want to go it alone. We
don't always agree on the line to follow, but everything will
sort itself out in the end, don't worry.

Christmas.

A pink Christ blubbering in his blanket.

Three decades with Man will cure him of fellow
feeling.

*I write these few lines to let you know how much I've
thought of you today. I felt a little blue earlier, but now
everything is much better and I'm in terrific spirits.* A new
letter from Fernand has arrived in the mail. *There's still
hope and I have a lot of it because I didn't kill or intend to
kill anyone, as the trial proved; I think this will be reviewed
with a cool head in France.* She stops, then continues. *My
sweet love, I end this letter here in the hope to read you soon
because for me your letters are the best medicine. Also many
kisses from the bottom of my heart.*

A mayor is felled by an FLN bullet. Straight to the
heart, inside his vehicle.

Arabs lynched in the streets, shops looted.

Flames and gunfire riddling the country's skin.

Monday, January 14: Bakri's sentence has been served.
Chikhi bids him farewell in Arabic. They hug. Fernand in
turn embraces him, good luck brother, be like the inmate
who's only a few minutes from not being one, it's going to

be alright you'll see, they'll get you out of here. Fernand smiles at him. He is glad, sincerely glad for him. Of course, he would love to be in his place, to leave these colorless walls and the death they promise, of course he would, but Bakri, dear Bakri, your good cheer helped me endure, it kept my head above water. Hug your family for me. Have children, Bakri, grow little heads upon this dirty earth, to wash out all the blood . . . The guard takes him, he turns around one last time with his same sunny smile, nods, the door is as gray as these damn walls, bye, Bakri.

One hour later, in comes registered number 5821.

Zamoun is the man's name, or that's how he introduces himself to Fernand and Chikhi. Like them he wears a jacket cut from a blanket, on the back of which are sewn the initials PCA (Prison Civile d'Alger). His pants are made of the same cloth, marked with a yellow cross. His face is long and narrow, his eyes tiny: sinister and sunken, like pin heads. His forehead is bare, his jaw prognathous and his teeth planted apparently at random, sprouting like weeds.

Twelve seconds is all it took, on the night of September 8, 1954, for Orléansville to collapse under the hammer of an earthquake.

Buildings bent over, roofs sundered, façades eviscerated, streets obstructed by telegraph poles or blocked by stones, schoolbooks scattered among the corpses . . . 1,500 dead, in no time or less, in the snap of a finger during a night which must have seemed, at first, exactly like all others— though some say (a singular omen) that cows and pigeons anticipated the tremors.

The church is open, gaping, its cross face down, its stomach spewing entrails of glass and wood; the Baudouin Hotel has spreadeagled over its clients, their skulls smashed by the walls which, minutes before, had protected them as they slept; the prison pierced from side to side. Like the aftermath of a massive bombardment, and yet no planes had passed above: these wings drilled in the deep. Debris and rubble under a stupefied dawn, heaps of blasted homes. A donkey lying against a car, an old man flattened

103

under dust and roof tiles, a young woman curled tight—no doubt for protection—under an uprooted tree . . .

Hélène and Fernand have come to help, with others from all over the country and sometimes from farther afield. The city is almost empty: the survivors fled, fearing a second wave of tremors. The heat is unbearable—more so for Hélène, who is not yet accustomed to the Algerian sun. Moist skin, sticky, uncomfortable clothes, sweat running down backs and foreheads. Pharmacists and doctors oversee the relief efforts—the army, firefighters, gendarmerie and police already, a few days ago, accomplished the "bulk" of this grim labor: evacuated the injured, gathered the bodies, searched for the missing under the ruins. Hélène is busy with a group of women volunteers (Algerian-Europeans and Muslims); Fernand distributes medication to all those who, traumatized by what they have seen or by the conditions in which they have since been forced to live, get in line to obtain what they need for themselves or their close ones, who may reside in Orléansville or the surrounding, equally affected villages. Hélène hands out food parcels during the day. Essential supplies—enough to hold out until a new roof is found.

As planned, Fernand left France in January. Cured. He looked for a home that could welcome Hélène and Jean-Claude, and finally found it, thanks to a friend of his father's, at 73 rue des Coquelicots—in his childhood neighborhood. He devoted all his leisure time to "patching it up," as he liked to say to his neighbors when announcing the arrival, more or less soon but in any case certain, of a "big surprise." He expected, and was even a little wary of it, that the change would be brutal for Hélène. At least their nest, their little den just for them, which however scarce their resources he'd planned and conceived as a cocoon, would allow her to find her feet, catch her breath between its cool walls, should the North African air be a bigger shock than she expected. Yet when she arrived in the first days of spring (early morning, traveled overnight), he had to acknowledge that his fears were unfounded: Hélène took to her new life at once. She had to make a few compromises, obviously, with local custom, and the strictness specific to those two cultures she was discovering for the first time: Muslim and "European." She understood that she could not smoke in public, unless she wanted to be thought a whore: a woman could not parade herself like that, cigarette in mouth, flagrant with smoke and indecency (Fernand was ashamed to admit that he cared about opinion, the rumors and the neighbors' stares, the gossips chattering in the shade of small courtyards; Hélène did not fail to point out that he had no issue with his "reputation" when it came to politics, even though his positions there were more dissonant than a simple smoke lit on the street). She liked the houses' pale whitewash and the sea, always present, unmistakable; she liked the pastries that people in the neighborhood offered her during Ramadan; she liked the Casbah's tortuous, rickety backstreets and its peppers, fish, citrus fruits, and severed sheep heads; she liked the archways in downtown Algiers and the Grande Poste's white elegance; she liked its harbor bristling with masts and piers, the gray swells of the Mediterranean; she liked the uprooted palm tree in their neighborhood, where passersby gathered to talk or relax; she also liked the kid, despite never learning his name, who asked for her hand one morning while she was going to the cobbler; she liked hearing that unknown Arabic tongue pour from windows, markets, cafés, rolling and billowing like cloth in dark mouths; she liked the interactions and collisions of a city between two worlds, Haussmann-style buildings and Moorish mosques, the strange face-to-face of colors and cultures.

What she did not like, however, was the daily arrogance she detected—or rather witnessed, since nothing was or is hidden—in the Europeans' dealings with the Muslims (she soon observed the verbal inventiveness humans can employ to describe those they do not wish to see amongst them: *crouilles, ratons, melons, bicots, bougnoules*). She was still amazed, months later, that seats in trolleybuses were never given up to Muslim women traveling with children. She also disliked the omnipotence of men, often Arab men, and their domination of public spaces (a presence that was never discussed or mentioned, as though it were normal, not to say "natural," to exclude women from the conversational arena—but in unspoken fashion, which perhaps made it more violent still, in that it was perfectly accepted and assimilated by all).

Fernand wanted her to stay at home, to enjoy the apartment and her new life, but she had other ideas. There was no reason she shouldn't be working and she was quick, soon after her arrival, to find a job—a couple, the husband an engineer, needed a maid. Jean-Claude came that summer, after finishing the school year in Seine-et-Marne. The change proved to be more difficult for the fourteen-year-old (who, if he thought well of Fernand, still could not bring himself to address him informally, as *tu*, to the latter's disappointment). He missed his friends. And quieter streets.

Hélène's family was at first somewhat baffled by the news. The famous "traite des Blanches," as the supposed traffic and forced prostitution of white women was known, was thought to be rampant in Arab lands. It scared her mother for a while, until all the family grew used to the idea of her living in Algeria, and even began to see the whole thing as a novel adventure. A bit of a thrill. Mystery and exoticism. Enough to keep the neighbors supplied with anecdotes, and so not without a certain pride.

We have just sent a letter to Guy Mollet, says Nordmann, protesting the tortures you suffered. You must now press charges on your own account. It's important for the case. I'll write it, you'll only have to sign. It'll be simpler that way, I'll send it to you. Fernand thanks him: he approves, of course. I don't know if you've heard (no, Fernand has not heard), but Djilali has been arrested. Shit, the prisoner blurts. And Jacqueline? Likewise. She confirmed that you didn't intend to kill anyone. Djilali's been transferred here, by the way, but I don't know where they put him. Maybe you'll pass each other in the yard . . . Fernand asks if he was tortured. Highly surprising if he wasn't, they beat up everything they can get their hands on. Fernand relates that the prison chaplain visits him regularly, and he enjoys their conversations. Those who believed in heaven and those who didn't, Nordmann murmurs. Sorry? It's a line from Aragon. Never read him. You should, his poetry is beautiful. I got to know him during the Occupation: one day I was instructed to give him some papers, which I concealed in my underwear, rolled up inside the seams. It was in Nice, a little house in the old part of Nice. I ring the bell, Elsa—his wife—opens. And there's Aragon. He had a luminous gaze. He'd heard nothing from the Party for months. Fernand interrupts, with apologies, to ask what those papers contained. Testimonies on hostage executions . . .

In his grandmother's study, Jean-Claude stamps an envelope: it holds the letter he is about to send to René Coty, at the Elysée, imploring him to save his stepfather. Pictured on the blue stamp is a man he knows nothing about: mustache and kepi, eyes fixed on a distant point. Underneath it says: Marshal Franchet d'Espèrey, born May 25, 1856 in Mostaganem, Algeria. No doubt, thinks Jean-Claude, the president knows who this person is—and if he is on this stamp, it's probably because he was a great man, which adds gravity to the request . . .

Zamoun arrived two weeks ago and has already been moved to another cell, promptly replaced by no. 400: Mohamed Ben Hamadi el Aziz—call me Abdelaziz, he tells his cellmates while firmly shaking their hands—an Iraqi who came to Algeria to fight with the Front. Captured after getting injured, a bullet to the groin. The military tribunal sentenced him to death. He imparts this lightly, almost serenely, in a low voice, almost suave. Abdelaziz, in addition to being a handsome man, is elegant. There is something of the prince about him, or a somber sire. The gaze is lively, two rings of black agate, convex eyelids as if drawn in charcoal. Short hair graying on a high forehead. The nose is long, hooked but harmonious, and the shapely beard chisels the already sharp outline of his features—it seems the man has self-esteem and cares about his appearance, though his situation is hardly conducive to grooming. His mouth (the lower lip distinctly more pronounced than the upper) purses sometimes, a kind of habit, when he finishes a sentence. He feels out the mattress. Takes his shoes off, straightens his back. Massages the back of his neck as if about to start warming up. Fernand observes him out of the corner of his eye—this man exudes something strange. It's probably what the word "aura" is for: not likability, he certainly does not inspire liking; not fear, either, he would refuse it. Something much more disquieting since it eludes the obvious, it slips away like sawdust in one's hand. The man is dashedly intelligent, his face corroborates it, but within his eyes and the set of his mouth, charm and harshness, sweetness and cruelty are at odds.

The wan blue of night. Not a cloud, not a star, not a ripple in sight—a motionless mass sprawled over the city. Abdelaziz, intrigued, asks Fernand—who is reading *Les Misérables*, a gift from the chaplain—if he too belongs to the Front in an official way. The three men are sat on their respective bunks. Fernand explains that he was originally an activist in the Algerian Communist Party and then joined its armed wing: the CDL, *Combattants de la Libération*. The FLN insurgency, at the end of '54, caused mayhem within the Party: activists were divided and the cadres did not know what stance to take. Was it a genuine revolution or the doing of reckless agitators, whose excessive radicality played right into the hands of the colonial authorities? Fernand had gotten fed up with the endless debates and procrastinations: Algeria was at war, they had to open their eyes, face up to reality and stop being afraid of confrontation. But they were repeatedly told to wait and, above all, respect the legal framework. Abdelaziz listens, his eyes narrowed like the arrowslits of a fortress. Fernand explains that he wanted to act with his comrades, lend a hand to the independentists, but the Party leaders remained silent . . . And then I lost someone close to me, a brother, a Frenchman. He was a soldier who deserted to join the guerrillas, stealing materiel belonging to the French army. He was shot . . . This pushed me to get even more involved. The FLN called for a general strike, I took part, as a factory worker. But the Party didn't budge from its position, it couldn't decide what to do: it was for independence, but not for armed struggle. But how else could independence be won, in this context? A deal was finally sealed between the Party and the FLN: communist militants could join the FLN, and hence the struggle, but only in a personal, individual capacity. That's what I did with my comrades. We had to prove ourselves before we could carry weapons and so, me and another guy (Fabien, but Fernand does not mention his name), we planned to set freight cars on fire in the harbor, after curfew. No one knows this, not even my wife, so I'm trusting you (Fernand feels that he can: Chikhi has a tongue between his teeth which he doesn't know how to use, and Abdelaziz didn't come from Iraq to rat on a cellmate): we had four bottles of gasoline, but when we got there, we saw armored cars . . . We weren't about to attack them with what we had! We turned back. Though we didn't agree with some of the FLN's methods, we were now under their orders. We didn't want to hurt civilians, that was out of the question. Killing is permissible during a war, but you kill soldiers or terrorists, not innocent bystanders. The next thing we did my wife doesn't know either: we tracked a guy, a member of an armed colonialist organization, a nut, a real brute. I was okay with shooting him, if I had to, but the operation fell through in the end. A comrade took down a military officer instead, a paratrooper (it is Hachelaf's name, this time, that Fernand withholds). I tell you all this, but at the same time I know where they come from, those bombs in cafés. I realize they don't come out of the blue, just look at the massacres committed by the army. But still, we're never going to find a solution by killing each other. Abdelaziz, who hadn't said a word, objects that pilots who bomb villages don't give a damn about the children cowering inside their homes—an eye for an eye, he concludes, his words as cutting as the blade he does not have on him, that'll keep those sons of swine in their place.

I know, I know, Fernand says, chilled by his interlocutor's impassive hatred, but that doesn't mean we should respond the same way . . . So, I offered to place a bomb in the factory where I work. An FLN leader—Yacef, you probably know him?—immediately thought of blowing up the lot, a mini Hiroshima, but I said that I didn't want to kill a single person, just make an impression on the colonialists, screw up some equipment. And now I'm here . . . Didn't the bomb kill anyone? the Iraqi asks. It didn't even explode. I was caught red-handed, so to speak. And you've been sentenced to death for that? Yes. Abdelaziz ponders at length before adding: you're French, they'll spare your life, don't worry about it. No, Fernand interjects, I'm Algerian. And Chikhi adds: even more than you are, Abdelaziz.

Smadja and Laînné arrive. They came to tell their client that they are going back to Paris to meet with President Coty. Laînné is confident: there's nothing about this case that would allow a pardon to be refused. Smadja does not contradict him, but Fernand senses that he's wary and uncomfortable. Laînné turns his rhinoceros-like body toward his colleague, isn't that right, Albert? Smadja nods. What about Nordmann, Fernand asks, will he be there with you? Yes, of course, there'll be three of us in front of the president. How could he not listen to us, with all that! Smadja asks the inmates whether they've been following recent events; Abdelaziz answers for all of them, and in the negative. Well, the FLN has decreed a general strike throughout Algiers, to get the UN's attention, put pressure on the next General Assembly. There's cops and soldiers everywhere, red and green berets. The Casbah is deserted. If the Arabs refuse to open their shops, the paratroopers will smash everything up. They're being forced to go back to work, corralled into stadiums, it's hell.

Fabien has been transferred to Barberousse.

They crossed each other on the way to the visiting room. Take heart, Fernand mumbled as he passed. The two men thought the exact same thing: how much the other had changed since they'd last met. Ravaged faces, bodies shrunken inside their clothes, and those dark circles, those faded veils under their eyes. Two specters in the entrails of Barberousse. The Nation—a face crawling with fleas. Back in his cell, Fernand wonders: does Fabien resent him? He must know, obviously, that his comrade betrayed him under beatings and electric shocks. Was Fabien braver than him? Fernand hopes so, at least.

Hélène . . .

A name like an itch. A wound in the roof of his mouth that he cannot forget.

He thinks of her every day. He cannot keep from doing it. Cannot keep from picking up the scattered pieces of their story, as if he had to put them in order between these walls, give them a meaning in this gray shithole, bulb on the ceiling, bunk stained by former inmates, one toilet between three. Give them a direction, a solid outline, thick, drawn in chalk or charcoal. Three and a half years together: one with the other, one through and for the other. Fernand collects whatever pieces his memory more or less readily restores to him, to form a brick—a cinder-block of love alone capable, in the face of an uncertain future, to break the bones and jaws of his tormentors.

Hélène.

Her blonde hair, the wonder of the neighborhood when she first came (everybody swore, rightly, that the Algerian sun would soon darken it). Her feet, which she said she once used to like, but not so much anymore. Her buttocks outlined under blue underwear, promising folds. The way people took her for Jean-Claude's older sister, since time washes over her without taking liberties (the very opposite of Fernand, who's always looked older than his age). Their wedding: Tuesday July 25, 1955, Algiers city hall. Afterward they danced most of the night away, with Jean-Claude, in a club near the racetrack. Their "lovely Sunday outings" as Hélène liked to call their excursions to Cherchell, near Tipaza. The song "Le Temps perdu," which Mathé Altéry had performed for France at Eurovision, a few months prior, in her high soprano, a song Hélène loved to play over and over . . .

For you, my love, he writes at the bottom of the letter he just finished.

Hélène is not so much hugging as carrying Fernand in her arms, for her husband's body has trouble holding itself up. He learned of Henri's death in the press. Like everyone else. Like so many strangers to whom this first and last name, Henri Maillot, meant nothing. Just another casualty, a line immediately forgotten, a few printed characters, dust to dust. Those in the know are already hailing the death of this "traitor"—others try to "understand what could've happened," of course, but "he was such a sweet man." Hélène is more shaken by the reaction of the man she loves than by the demise of a man she hardly knew: it is the first time she's seen Fernand like this, overcome by spasms, quivering with tears, incapable of finding the words to articulate what his eyes can only stutter. She says nothing but understands perfectly well what led Henri to act as he did. She herself had told Fernand, after discovering Algeria: when the French had had enough of the Germans, they took to the maquis, period. She agreed with him on this point enough to have allowed, last year, a

117

few men to stay in their house—men of whom all she knew was that the police or the army was after them.

Hélène was struck, on meeting Henri for the first time, by the gulf which drew the two friends together: the energy of the one reaching out to the other's calm, the spontaneity of the worker reaching out to the accountant's reserve. Those who found him cold sensed nothing of his inner fire, his quiet, subterranean strength, sources made more formidable by his refusal to give outsiders a glimpse of them. Henri loved an Arab woman, Baya, who loved him back. She had been married against her will to a cousin, at the age of fourteen, and became a mother a year later: she managed to separate from her husband at the age of twenty and did as she pleased from then on, liberating herself from the veil and stuffing her head with communist texts. Henri worked for the daily *Alger républicain*, and Fernand knew that his comrades appreciated him for his seriousness and efficiency: the man always filed his stories before the deadline.

He shaved with care and cut his curly hair short over his big, rounded forehead. His gaze was subtle, almost feminine. His eyes were lively and intense; they fixed his interlocutor without ever betraying his thoughts. A long nose, sharp and protruding like the frame of his face. Henri attracted women without realizing it: his calm was not a form of stillness, but rather a purity, like that of high mountain lakes. His moderation was only apparent. His anger, which was rare, had more in common with fury—like the day he told Abdelhamid, a journalist friend, of how in Constantine a paratrooper captain had shoved his revolver, after wiping the barrel with a tissue, into the mouth of an Algerian baby and pulled the trigger. Henri had howled. He swore that it was necessary to kill every paratrooper, one by one. That they had to rip this whole system up—that he would never forget what he'd seen, those decomposing Arab bodies floating in the Oued Rhumel. Abdelhamid had listened in silence on that occasion.

Toward the end of 1955, he enlisted as a cadet in a battalion of the French army, and was tasked a few months later with transporting weapons from Miliana to Algiers: he pointed his own at the truck driver—they were ferrying 140 handguns, grenades, magazines, as well as 132 machine guns—and forced him into a forest of pine and eucalyptus trees where communist comrades, informed of the operation beforehand, were waiting. The driver was chloroformed; the whole cargo was stolen. Henri had kissed his sister before leaving, divulging nothing, of course, about his plans. His desertion shook Algeria as much as it did France, and he was sentenced to death. Meanwhile his group turned into a maquis or guerrilla unit, fighting the French army but without, at the same time, joining the ranks of the FLN. The independentists were soon attacked and Henri was captured alive by soldiers of the 504 BT: after beating him up, they told him he was free to go. He knew it wasn't true and walked backwards, shouting "Long live the Algerian Communist Party!" until they shot him dead.

His body was driven into town on the hood of an armored vehicle, his hair dyed with henna, false papers in his pockets. A trophy for a great victory.

Civilization puffs its chest, brandishing rod and flag.

Marianne trades in her tricolor nights—swapping pennies for chimeras.

I am not Muslim, Henri had written shortly before, *but I am a European Algerian. I consider Algeria to be my country. I must fulfill toward it the same duties as all of its sons. As soon as the Algerian people rose up to free their land from under the colonial yoke, I knew my place was alongside those engaged in the fight for liberation. The colonial press shouts treason, while at the same time it publishes and endorses the separatist calls of Boyer and Banse. It also cried treason when, under Vichy, French officers joined the Resistance, while it was serving Hitler and fascism. In truth, the traitors to France are those who, to serve their own selfish interests, pervert in the eyes of Algerians the true face of France and of its people, whose traditions are generous, revolutionary, and anticolonial. What's more, every progressive man in France and in the world recognizes the legitimacy and justice of our national claims. The Algerian people, long thwarted and humiliated, have taken their resolute place in the great historic movement of colonial liberation, a movement which has set Africa and Asia ablaze. Its victory is certain. And this is not, as the biggest owners of wealth in this country would have us believe, a racial conflict, but a struggle of the oppressed, without distinction of origins, against the oppressors and their valets, without distinction of race. This is not a movement aimed against France and the French, or against workers of French or Israelite origin. These have their place in this country. We do not confuse them with our people's oppressors. In my actions, in giving*

to Algerian fighters the weapons they need for their libera-
tion, weapons which will be used exclusively against military
and police forces, as well as against collaborators, I am
conscious of having served my country and my people,
including those European workers who were momentarily
deceived.

Fernand catches his breath.

Hélène wipes one of his cheeks with the palm of her hand. She could have licked his face until the tears stopped falling, this beautiful puppet, its strings cut by distress.

We have to act, he finally whispers. Do something. So he won't have died for nothing.

René Coty wears a dark pinstriped suit. He has flat hair combed to the left, protruding ears and a nose like a lump of bread. Nordmann, Smadja and Laînné are sat on the three chairs positioned in front of his desk in the Elysée. The president of the Republic appears smiling and gracious. Benevolent, even. After listening to the three lawyers recapitulate the grave failings they wish to stress (the climate of collective hysteria in Algeria, the impossibility of prior investigation and preparation by the defense, the torture undergone by their client, the impartial brutality of the press), Coty assures them that he is familiar with the case, and that he too considers the sentence out of proportion to the allegations. He even discerns a dash of nobility there—or at least he can, while disapproving of Iveton's action, recognize the courage of his intentions and the element of charity in his motives. But all this reminds me of another story, he continues. In 1917, when I was a young officer, thirty-five years old, something like that, I witnessed with my own eyes the execution of two young

French soldiers. As one of them was being taken to the wall, the general said to him, I remember it perfectly: you too, my son, you die for France. He pauses after these words. Smadja hears what he did not say, or thinks he does, interpreting as follows: Coty, in mentioning this unfortunate soldier, is contemplating Fernand Iveton: he too, then, is about to die for France. Coty resumes, explaining that the appeals for a pardon he has received from Algeria are significantly outnumbered by the calls for the sentence to be carried out. And there is the matter of public order, he adds. Nordmann cuts in: with all due respect, *monsieur le président*, this argument doesn't hold water. To guillotine Iveton would certainly satisfy the spirit of blind retaliation, but believe me, believe us, it will not in the least intimidate the Arab population. They will keep fighting with whatever means at their disposal, do not doubt it, *monsieur*. Nordmann pushes on in a firm, fluent voice, without bother: when I was cabinet director at the Justice Ministry during the liberation of Paris, I myself wrote and put up posters calling on the population to abstain from summary executions. Blind violence solves nothing, nothing at all. Coty listens attentively, a little leather notebook in front of him. He makes occasional jottings in it. Allow me to tell you an anecdote: when one of the prison guards insulted our client, do you know how he reacted? "You fool, I'm in here for your sake!" Yes, take note of that, *monsieur le président*. Our client is conscious of fighting for more than himself. He's fighting for his country, which he wants to see free and happy, a country which guarantees to each and every one of its citizens, Muslim or European, freedom of thought and equality. Our client wants nothing else. Smadja takes a letter out of his bag, signed by Hélène and addressed to René Coty. The president takes it, promises to read it without delay and puts it down to his right, on top of a thick folder labeled "Fernand Ivcton." And Laînné insists: our client must be heard as a witness, especially with regard to the torture he suffered. The president concurs—it is indeed unworthy of the police or army of the Republic to have behaved in such a fashion, should the alleged acts be confirmed. The interview has lasted an hour and a half. The four men give each other their regards. Coty sees them to his office door.

What to make of it? The lawyers are not sure. Smadja is the most definite: he's not going to pardon him—the story about the soldier proves it. Do you think? Yes, quite certain, bet my life on it. Tomorrow, Wednesday, February 6, the High Council of the Judiciary will examine the case again.

By a certified letter in Nordmann's handwriting, Fernand has received a report on the meeting. He immediately responds: *I know that I can trust the people of France; please give them my fraternal regards at every chance you get, with my thanks and in the hope that I may do it in person some not too distant day. I believe, in view of the account of your visit to the President of the Republic in your letter, that I have some chance. And so I thank you with all my heart, with the conviction that I will see you again as a free man.*

Saturday. Chikhi is free. He has served his sentence. He shakes Abdelaziz's hand, puts his hand on his heart and hugs Fernand in silence. Don't say anything, brother, he whispers, God will know what you have done for our country. He had assembled his belongings the day before. The guard waits for him and then closes the door. Four to five hours later, it opens again. A young Arab, not yet twenty years old, enters. Achouar. Another CAM. Arrested during a firefight with the French army, at Tighremt: he asked to be given the status of prisoner of war. The hunting rifle in his hands was still hot. His face is sweet, almost childish. Fernand asks him immediately if he knows anything about the death of Henri Maillot, eight months ago now, last June. No, nothing. He's heard the name, everybody has, the Frenchman who fought side by side with Algerians, but that's all.

They spend most of the night in conversation.

Ten in the morning. Time to go for a walk. Fernand follows his guard like he does every day, handcuffed, every damn day these last three prison-bound months. The CAM yard is smaller than that of other inmates. Fernand paces back and forth. Soles on gray cement. Several men are on watch. A few faces, occasionally familiar, are sketched out in stripes behind the window bars; Fernand waves at some with his hobbled hands. He goes back to the cell. Abdelaziz is doing abdominal exercises while Achouar meticulously cleans his shoes with toilet paper. The minute he comes in, sits down and picks up *Les Misérables* at the page he left it, Laînné and Smadja arrive. Fernand is glad to see them, and shows it. He tells them he has heard from Nordmann and dares to hope, even now, that he might be pardoned. Coty is sure to make the right decision. Isn't he? Smadja tries his best to conceal his total lack of hope.

126

Meaning to smile, he makes a sour face—which betrays him to the man he wants to fool. Laînné strives to be more reassuring, he shakes his bovine head: the president didn't say anything one way or the other, but let's hope so, indeed, cross our fingers while we wait for the verdict. Imminent. Any day now. None of the three lawyers have mentioned Coty's story about the soldier who was executed for France . . . They withdraw for the lunch hour. Give my love to Hélène if you see her before she visits me, adds Fernand as he gets up to say goodbye.

The food is lukewarm today. Pasta and beef, like every Sunday. A sauce uncertain in color, opaque at depth. Fernand bolts the meal, eager to return to his reading. *Jean Valjean was not dead. When he fell into the sea, or rather when he threw himself into it, he was not ironed, as we have seen. He swam under water until he reached a vessel at anchor, to which a boat was moored. He found means of hiding himself in this boat until night. At night he swam off again, and reached the shore a little way from Cape Brun . . .* Two bombs tear into the afternoon in the Algiers stadiums of El-Biar and Ruisseau. Ten dead, thirty or so injured, blood everywhere, wounds and mutilations. Two random passersby, unlucky enough to be Arabs, were lynched by an angry mob. Night slips over the city, a thick veil of silent mourning. Jean Valjean watches Cosette as she sleeps, feeds her, protects her, teaches her to read. He has come to see the world and mankind differently since loving Cosette. Fernand bids his two companions good-night. His tired eyes have trouble following the slack, wavering lines, but he means to keep on reading. Just a little more. Two or three pages. *Jean Valjean knew no more where he was going than did Cosette. He trusted in God, as she trusted in him. It seemed as though he was also clinging to the hand of some one greater than himself; he thought he felt a being leading him, though invisible. However, he had no settled idea, no plan, no project. He was not even absolutely sure that it was Javert, and then it might have been Javert, without Javert knowing that he was Jean Valjean. Was not he disguised? Was not he believed to be dead?* His eyelids won't stay open. He puts the work down after book-marking his page with a canteen coupon, then turns on his side, in the fetal position, since he never could (and always wondered how others did) fall asleep on his back, flat out, staring at the ceiling. He sinks after a few minutes, without even realizing it. And suddenly noise, lights. The adverb, in truth, does little more than conceal the confusion that seizes Fernand: he opens his eyes, not sure where he is, what time is it, what's all this noise, is he dreaming or what? He turns his head, what time is it, I was sleeping, guards, guards, shit, what's all this noise? Guards are standing over him, sure enough, against the light of a white bulb. They tell him to get up immediately. Fernand does not understand. Abdelaziz is up, frowning: he understands everything. This way, Iveton. Your pardon was denied. Get up, now. Fernand complies. Stunned. Astounded. The brain still heavy with sleep. He is in his underwear and asks to put his pants on: one of the guards refuses, curtly. He is pushed. On the threshold he turns around and looks at Achouar and Abdelaziz. The first seems lost, haggard, perhaps even more so than Fernand; the second is grave, immovable, an ancient statue: his black eyes have severed at a stroke the fumes of sleep. Those sharp black eyes, beyond doubt, compel the convict to open his own, for good, this time. Brothers . . . says Fernand, but a hand is instantly clapped over his mouth, yanks him backwards. Panicking, Achouar asks what's going on; Abdelaziz does not answer. He is looking at the ceiling, lying down on his bunk. Fernand is hustled through the corridor. Dawn stirs, shakes its yellow folds. It is almost five. Headlights outside, the sound of a moving gate, of vehicles . . . The prisoners of Barberousse sense that something unusual is afoot. As he makes his way, Fernand slowly begins, from scattered fragments, to piece it all together. Coty, Mitterrand, and the rest denied his pardon, his head will fall. He thinks of Hélène. Of Henri. Stand tall, like them. He hollers into the passageways: *Tahia El Djazaïr* (Long Live Algeria)! Once. He hollers so as not to collapse or cry. A second time. *Tahia El Djazaïr!* A guard tells him to shut it and holds a baton to his waist. Voices answer him already, voices which understand it all. He is taken to the prison registry. Yells, in Arabic, chants and slogans surround him, not that he is able to tell where they are coming from. They bounce behind him, sometimes a long way, bump together inside his beleagured head. The prison flexing its muscles. His temples buzz. *Tahia El Djazaïr! Tahia El Djazaïr!* The screws are suddenly dizzy, if not panicked: the prisoners, despite their confinement, are slipping away—their hopes knocking down the iron doors. There is no heart the state can constrain; dreams eat into its reason like acid. The registrar asks Fernand whether he has anything to say before the start of the proceedings. He answers that he would like to put on a pair of pants. He then tells this honest civil servant, so that he may write it down: "The life of a man, my life, matters little. What matters is Algeria, its future. And tomorrow Algeria will be free. I am convinced that the friendship between the French and the Algerians will be mended." That's all. The registrar thanks him. He is given a pair of pants and canvas shoes. He is putting them on when two Arab men enter, escorted by a few guards. Mohamed Lakhnèche, also known as Ali Chaflala, and Mohamed Ouenouri, alias P'tit Maroc. Fernand realizes that they are to be executed with him. The prisoners are hitting the walls of their cells with metal bowls and spoons. The prison's lungs fill up, inhale, exhale. In the surrounding streets, women are now shouting from their windows, supporting the combatants. Ululations, patriotic chants, and *nachîds*. ينادينا للاستقلال، لاستقلال وطننا The three convicts enter the yard. تضحيتنا للوطن خير من الحياة The guillotine looms proudly on the cement floor. There is the slanted blade, odious, there is the hole, round hole, perfectly round. أضحّي بحياتي وبمالي عليك Ululations submerge, overflow and saturate the area. Smadja, Laînné and Father Declercq are present. They were waiting. Fernand is surprised to see them—he does not know, in fact, that his lawyers were told the previous afternoon, by telephone. The air is not cold; it is even rather mild. يا بلادي يا بلادي، أنا لا أهوى سواك Five o'clock. Laînné embraces Fernand, bc strong, he whispers, it's because of public opinion. You are French, you placed a bomb somewhere, to them that's unforgivable: you are to die because of public opinion. Fernand's stomach feels as if it is being lacerated, clawed, pierced by a thousand lead pellets. قـد سـلا الدنيـا فـؤادي وتفانـى فـي هـواك Fernand repeats it three times, public opinion public opinion public opinion. He finds it hard to breathe. The Casbah calls the sky to itself in screams and ululations, an unbroken thread of sound. He is brought to the executioner, who wears a hood. Fernand does not know that this masked man, nicknamed "Monsieur d'Alger," is also called Fernand. The executioner, hearing the convict's name uttered by the chaplain, catches himself flinching. As if death were finally embodied—after all the heads he's dispatched with a most professional hand—in the sound of a first name which returns him, brutally, to their common humanity. Declercq asks him whether he requires the succor of religion; Fernand looks at him, tries to smile, fails, and answers no . . . no . . . freethinker . . . لـك في التاريـخ ركن مشـرف فـوق السـماك The guards bind his hands behind his back. I am going to die, he murmurs, but Algeria will be independent . . . Fernand goes first: custom dictates that the least "guilty" convict opens the proceedings, so that he need not witness others being put to death. His two lawyers withdraw to one of the corridors leading off the yard. Laînné kneels, bows his head, joins his hands together toward his Lord. Smadja stands, in tears, forehead against the wall. They do not want to look, they cannot. It is 05:10 when the head of Fernand Iveton, prisoner number 6101, thirty years old,

Hélène folds the letter in half. Then in four. Anonymous. Only a postscript, in which she learns that the author of this poem, written in memory of Fernand, is a European-Algerian woman, a militant for independence sentenced to five years in prison.

Then the cock crowed
This morning they dared to
They dared to murder you.

In the fortress of our bodies
May our ideal live on
Mingled with your blood
So that tomorrow they won't dare,
They won't dare to murder us.

In the historiography of François Mitterrand
and the Algerian War, Iveton remains a cursed
name. [. . .] One has to wonder how President
Mitterrand could own up to it. I must have
uttered the name [of Iveton] two or three
times in front of him, always to his terrible
unease, which then turned into eructations.
[. . .] One had run into the raison d'État.

B. Stora and F. Malye,
François Mitterrand et la guerre d'Algérie

Guillotined on February 11, 1957, Fernand Iveton is the
only "European" to have been executed by France during
the Algerian War. In its coverage of his death, *France-Soir*, a leading newspaper, described him as a "killer."
Paris-Presse, another mainstream organ, called him a
"terrorist."

Two days after Iveton's beheading, Albert Smadja was arrested and taken to the Lodi internment camp, set up to "silence those who may denounce the repression, get in contact with arrested militants, support their families and friends, or hamper the prosecution during their trials":[1] he was liberated toward the end of 1958. Two years later, that is. In March of that year, Jean-Paul Sartre published a text to the memory of Iveton in *Les Temps modernes*.[2]

André Abbou, author of *Albert Camus, entre les lignes*,[3] claims that the novelist "intervened" to try to save him.[4] The Guerroudj couple was pardoned by de Gaulle— Jacqueline died in Algiers at the age of ninety-five (a few weeks before the start of the writing of this book). Hélène Iveton and Fernand's father left Algeria without delay; she died on Sunday, May 10, 1998 in Arcueil. Joë Nordmann discussed the case in his memoir, *Aux vents de l'histoire*.[5]

In his *Coups et blessures*, the socialist politician Roland Dumas maintains that if François Mitterrand moved to abolish the death penalty in 1981, as soon as he came to power, it was in order to "redeem" himself for the

1 See Nathalie Funès, *Le Camp de Lodi*, Stock, 2012.

2 Jean-Paul Sartre, "Nous sommes tous des assassins," *Les Temps modernes* 145 (1958).

3 André Abbou, *Albert Camus, entre les lignes*, Séguier, 2009.

4 "But it is too late, and all that is left to do is either repent or forget. Of course, we forget. Society, however, is no less affected. Unpunished crimes, according to the Greeks, infected the city-state." Albert Camus on Iveton, in "Réflexions sur la guillotine," *Nouvelle Revue française* 54 and 55 (June– July 1957).

5 Joë Nordmann, *Aux vents de l'histoire*, Actes Sud, 1999.

decisions he took during the Algerian War, including Iveton's execution.[6]

These pages could not have been written without the patient investigative work of Jean-Luc Einaudi. He has left us, but I thank him here. He reported that throughout his investigation he was met with nothing but "the silence of the State."[7]

6 Roland Dumas, *Coups et blessures*, Le Cherche-Midi, 2011.
7 See Jean-Luc Einaudi, *Pour l'exemple. L'affaire Fernand Iveton*, L'Harmattan, 1986.